Ocean of Words

Ha Jin

Ocean of Words

ARMY STORIES

Z

ZOLAND BOOKS
Cambridge, Massachusetts

First edition published in 1996 by
Zoland Books
384 Huron Avenue
Cambridge, Massachusetts 02138

FIRST EDITION

Book design by Boskydell Studio

Printed in the United States of America

02 01 00 99 98 97 96   8 7 6 5 4 3 2

This book is printed on acid-free paper, and its binding
materials have been chosen for strength and durability.

Library of Congress Cataloging-in-Publication Data
Jin, Ha, 1956-
Ocean of words : army stories / Ha Jin. — 1st ed.
p.   cm.
ISBN 0-944072-58-5 (alk. paper)
1. China.   Chung–kuo jen min chieh fang chün—Fiction.
2. Soldiers—China—Social life and customs—Fiction   I. Title
PS3560.I6024   1996
813'.54—dc20   95-43974
CIP

TO MY TEACHER

Leslie Epstein

ACKNOWLEDGMENTS

"Love in the Air" has appeared in *Yellow Silk;*
"My Best Soldier" in *AGNI, The Pushcart
Prize (XVII)* and *Literatures of Asia, Africa,
and Latin America* (Barnstore and Barnstore,
eds.); winner of the AGNI Best
Fiction Prize (1991); "The Russian Prisoner"
in *Witness;* "Dragon Head" in *AGNI;*
"Ocean of Words" in *Chelsea.*

Contents

Ocean of Words

A Report

Our Most Respected Divisional Commissar Lin:

I am writing to report on an event that occurred last Saturday afternoon. Our Reconnaissance Company, the best trained men and the flower of our Second Division, marched through Longmen City to the Western Airport, where we were to do parachute exercises. While we were passing Central Boulevard at the corner of the First Department Store, I ordered Scribe Hsu Fang to start a song with an eye to impressing the pedestrians. He executed the orders, and the whole company began to sing:

> Good-bye, mother, good-bye, mother —
> The battle bugle blowing,
> Steel guns shiny,
> The outfits on our backs,
> Our army is ready to go.
> Please do not weep in secret,
> Please do not worry about your son.
> Wait for my triumphant return;
> I will see you then, my dear mother.
> . . . . . .

While we were singing, the march suddenly slowed down, and the uniform footsteps of one hundred men grew disordered. The words and music, suitable only for lamentation, melted the strength in the soldiers' feet. I shouted to stop the singing, which in fact became crying. But we were in the middle of the thoroughfare, and my voice could not overcome the loud noises of the bustling traffic, so they continued to sing. Some new soldiers burst out sobbing; even the experienced ones were overwhelmed with tears. Imagine, a hundred of the best-disciplined fighters were bleating without shame on the street like a herd of sheep! And with machine guns and bazookas! People paused on the sidewalks to watch us whining and weeping. Someone commented, "This is a funeral procession."

I do not blame my men, nor have I criticized Scribe Hsu Fang. They are brave soldiers, and the history of our company has borne that out with ample evidence. Our Most Esteemed Commissar Lin, probably I am partly responsible for this occurrence, because I did not prevent my men from learning the song in the first place. My vigilance of class struggle must have slackened. I thought it would do them no harm if they sang a song that the Central Radio Station broadcast every day. Please do not misunderstand me here: We did not teach this contagious song; the soldiers just learned it by themselves. My mistake was not to intervene in time.

The event I have described demonstrates that this song is a counterrevolutionary one. All the men in my company now feel ashamed, because they were seized by the surprise of bourgeois sentiment. We have all been dishonored and have done damage to the image of our army.

It goes without saying that a true revolutionary song belongs to the kind that inspires, unifies, and instructs, not like the one we sang, which undermines our morale and destroys our solidarity. A good song must encourage people's upright spirit and must make friends more lovable and enemies more detestable. Commissar Lin, you must remember those old genuine revolutionary fighting songs; here I cannot help picking out one as an example:

> We are all super marksmen.
> Every bullet strikes an enemy dead.
> We are all swift troops,
> Not afraid of waters deep and mountains high.
> On the lofty cliffs
> There are our quarters.
> In the thick woods
> There are many good brothers.
> If we have no clothes and food
> The enemy sends them to us.
> If we have no weapons
> The enemy makes them for us.
> We were born and grew up here,
> Every inch of the land is ours.
> If someone dares to take it from us,
> We shall fight him to the end!

What a song! At this very moment of writing, I can recall that when singing it we walked with tremendous confidence, as if the earth beneath our feet would quake because of us and as if we could topple the mountains and overturn the seas, not to mention eliminate our enemies. I need not dwell on this further, because you, a Revolutionary of the Older Generation, actually grew up with those genuine songs, and you must have a profounder understanding of their nature than I do.

The lesson we have learned from the reported event is as follows: Our class enemies are still active, and they never go to sleep; whenever we doze off, they will take advantage of us, sabotaging Socialism and changing the political color of our army. We must grow another pair of eyes in the backs of our heads so that we can keep them under watch everywhere and at all times.

Our Most Respected Comrade Commissar, on behalf of

my company, I suggest we ban this poisonous song and investigate the family and political backgrounds of its author and its composer. Whoever they are, they undoubtedly have the outlook of the bourgeoisie. They have committed sabotage — their work aims to disable our troops, corroding the iron bastion from within. Also, those who have helped disseminate this song must not be let off their responsibility. Ideally, we should bring a couple of people to the Military Court. We must show our enemies that we are also superior fighters on the Ideological Front!

My Revolutionary Salute,

I Remain Your Loyal Soldier,
Political Instructor and
Party Secretary of
Reconnaissance Company —
Chen Jun
Longmen, May 27

Too Late

It began as a bet at the Spring Festival. After the feast, the soldiers of my company were playing chess and poker, chatting and cracking roasted peanuts and sunflower seeds. In the Second Platoon some men were talking about women and bragging of their own ability to resist female charms. Gradually their topic shifted to the Shanghai girls at the Youth Home in Garlic Village. How were the girls doing on the holiday eve? What a pity there was no man in their house. Who would dare to go have a look and ask if they miss their parents and siblings?

Someone said he would pay a Spring Festival call on the girls after eleven. Another boasted that he would take a bottle of wine to that house and have a cup with them. Emboldened by alcohol and the festive atmosphere, they indulged themselves in the big talk.

Then Kong Kai declared he dared to go and sleep on the same brick bed with the girls. This was too much. Everybody thought he just wagged his tongue, and they told him to draw a line somewhere if he wanted to talk sense. But a few men challenged him and even proposed a five-*yuan* bet. To their amazement, Kong swung his quilt roll on his back and set off for the Youth Home.

There was only one young man living at that house, but he had left to spend the holiday with his family in Shanghai. Unlike the country women, those city girls had tender limbs and looked rather elegant. They knew how to use makeup and wore colorful clothes.

Kong entered the Youth Home and dropped his quilt at the end of the brick bed. The five girls were too shocked to stop him. He climbed on the bed, spread his quilt, lay down, and closed his eyes. For half an hour, they didn't know what to do about this man, who wouldn't respond to their questioning and tittering and instead was sleeping or pretending to be asleep. They brought out candies, chocolates, and frozen pears in the hope of inducing him to open his mouth, which like his eyes was shut all the time. They even cooked him a large bowl of dragon-whiskers noodles with garlic, ginger, and two poached eggs, hoping the fragrance might arouse his appetite. Nothing worked. One of them put a few lamp-soot stains on his face, saying, "This makes him look more handsome." They giggled; still he remained motionless. Finally, the five girls decided to keep watch on him by turns throughout the night, for fear he might do something unusual once they went to sleep, though they knew Kong by sight and didn't feel he was a bad man. Each of them sat beside him for one and a half hours while the rest were sleeping at the other end of the large bed. The oil lamp was burning until dawn.

On hearing of the incident at daybreak, Commander Deng and I set out for Garlic Village right away. It was crisply cold, and a large flock of crows were gliding over the snow-covered fields, clamoring hungrily. A few firecrackers exploded in the village that sprawled ahead like a deserted battlefield. Among some wisps of cooking smoke, two roosters were crowing on and on, as if calling each other names. In the north, the Wusuli River almost disappeared in the snow, and beyond it a long range of cedar woods stretched on the hillside like a gigantic spearhead pointing to the Russians' watchtower, which was wavering in the clouds. Though day was unfolding, the Russians' searchlight kept flickering.

When we arrived Kong was still in bed. The girls were all up, some washing clothes while others were combing and braiding their hair. They looked jubilant, humming light tunes and giggling as if something auspicious had descended on their household. At the sight of us they stopped.

"Lock up the door and don't let anyone out," Commander Deng cried. With a mitten he wiped the frost off his mustache, his deep-sunk eyes glinting. He spat a cigarette end to the floor and stamped it out. Orderly Zhu executed the orders.

Kong Kai heard the noise and got out of bed to meet us. He didn't look worried and gave us a toothy grin. His broad face was smeared with soot, but he still had on his fur hat, whose earflaps were tied together under his chin. I felt relieved; it seemed he hadn't taken off his clothes during the night. We brought him into the inner room and began our questioning.

It took us only a few minutes to finish with him. He tried to convince us that he had slept well. That must have been a lie. How could a young man sleep peacefully while a girl was sitting nearby with her eyes on him all the time? And another four sleeping on the same bed? Didn't he know his face still had stains of lamp soot on it? But we didn't ask him those questions, for it wasn't important for us to know how he had felt and what he knew. We cared only what he had done.

Convinced that nothing serious had taken place, we put him aside and brought in the girls one by one. Each questioning was shorter than two minutes. "Did he touch you?" Deng asked a tall, pale-faced girl, whom we had got hold of first.

"No." She shook her head.

"Did he say anything to you?"

"Un-un."

"Yes or no?"

"No."

"Did he ever take off his clothes?"

"No."

In the same manner we went through the other four girls, who gave us identical answers. Then we brought our man home, believing the case was closed. On the way back I criticized Kong briefly for intruding into a civilian house without any solid reason, especially on the Spring Festival's Eve, when the Russians were most likely to cross the border and nobody was allowed to leave the barracks.

At once Kong became a hero of a sort. Those foolish boys called him "an iron man." Together with his fame, numerous versions of his night adventure were circulating in the company. One even said that the girls had welcomed Kong's arrival and lain beside him by turns throughout the night, patting his face, murmuring seductive words, and even drawing a thick mustache on his lip with charcoal, but the iron man hadn't budged a bit, as though he were unconscious. We tried to stop them from creating these kinds of silly stories and assured them that the girls were fine, not as bad as they thought. They'd better cleanse their own minds of dirty fantasies.

A month later Kong's squad leader, Gu Chong, was transferred to the battalion headquarters, to command the antiaircraft machine gun platoon there. Gu suggested we let Kong take over the Fifth Squad. Indeed Kong seemed to be an ideal choice; the men in our company respected him a lot, and he was an excellent soldier in most ways. So we promoted him to squad leader.

Who could tell "the iron man" would be our headache? In a few weeks it was reported that Kong often sneaked out in the evenings and on weekends to meet a girl at the Youth Home. There were larch woods at the eastern end of Garlic Village; it was said that Kong and the girl often wandered in the woods. I talked to him about this. He said they had gone in there only to pick mushrooms and daylilies. What a lie. I told him to stop pretending. Who would believe the iron man had become a mushroom picker accompanied by a girl? I wanted him to quit the whole thing before it was too late, and I reminded him of the discipline that allowed no soldier to have an affair.

One Sunday morning in April, Orderly Zhu reported that Kong had disappeared from the barracks again. Immediately I set out with Scribe Yang for the larch woods. When we got there we came upon two lines of fresh footprints on the muddy slope. We followed them. Without much difficulty we found the lovers, who were sitting together by a large rock. They saw us approaching, and they got up and slipped away into the woods. We walked over and found five golden candy wrappers at the spot. I told the scribe to pick up the wrappers, and together we returned.

Scribe Yang said he recognized the girl, whose name was An Mali. The tall, pale-faced one, he reminded me. I recalled questioning her and didn't feel she was a bad girl at all, but a rule was a rule, which no one should break. Kong was creating trouble not only for himself but also for our company. We had to stop him.

Soon the leader of the Second Platoon reported that there had been confrontations between Kong and some men in the Fifth Squad. One soldier openly called him "womanizer."

In May we held the preliminary election of exemplary soldiers. As usual, we had all the guns and grenades and bazookas locked away at the company's headquarters for five days, for fear somebody might be so upset about not being elected that he would resort to violence. There had

9

been bloodshed during the election in other units, and we had to take precautions.

All the squad leaders were voted in except Kong Kai, though three of his men got elected. The soldiers complained that Kong had a problematic life-style. Commander Deng and I worried about the results of the election, particularly about Kong, so we decided to talk to him.

After taps, we had him summoned to our office. The kerosene lamp on the desk was shining brighter with the new wick Orderly Zhu had put in. I walked to the window to look out at the moonlit night while Deng read a newspaper at the desk. Beside his elbow lay a blue notebook and a pen; whenever he came across a new word, he would write it down. He had only three years' education.

In the distance a Russian helicopter was flickering and hammering away among the stars. The hills beyond the border loomed like huge graves. I was wondering how Kong had started the affair. When we had questioned him and the girls three months before, we had been quite certain nothing had happened to him. How did the seed of love enter his brain? Was it because she had smeared lamp soot on his face?

Kong's stocky body emerged on the drill ground coming to the headquarters. I returned to the desk and sat down by Deng. "Take a seat, Little Kong," I said the moment he stepped in.

Straight to the point, we asked him what he thought of the election, and he admitted he felt bad about being voted out. His almond eyes kept flashing at us. I handed him a cigarette, which he declined.

"Three months ago," Deng said, "you were 'an iron man' in your comrades' eyes, but all of a sudden you become a womanizer to them. How can you explain the change?"

"I'm not a womanizer."

"Let's get this straight," I said. "When we picked you up

at the Youth Home, you said you hadn't done anything with the girls. Did you lie to us?"

"No, I didn't."

"Then how did you hit it off with An Mali?" Deng asked.

Kong remained silent, biting his bottom lip.

"Little Kong," I resumed, "there must have been something between you two which you've hidden from us."

"No, I didn't hide anything. I didn't know it when we came back together."

"Know what?" Deng said.

"The note. She left a note in my breast pocket. I didn't know it till three days later."

"Let's have a look at it." Deng stretched out his hand, and Kong slowly took out his wallet and produced the note. Deng read it and then passed it to me and cursed, "Bitch."

On the scrap of yellow paper there were these few words:

I know you. Your name is Kong Kai. — An Mali.

No one could say that was a secret message or a love note, so I said to Kong, "There's nothing unusual in this. It doesn't explain the affair."

"I was curious to see how she knew my name."

"So you went back to her?" Deng said.

"Yes."

"Shame on you two!"

I didn't feel the girl was in the wrong. Kong was the one who had broken into the Youth Home and then gone back to look for her, so he should be held responsible. However, it would be impracticable to order him to cut the affair at one stroke. He was a man and should break it off on his own initiative, so I switched the topic a little by asking him how he was going to make sure he would be elected an exemplary soldier at the end of the year. He said he would try every way to gain enough votes. We knew that was an empty promise, for as long as he was carrying on the affair, he had no chance of being voted in. Commander Deng got impatient and said, "Comrade Kong Kai, you know, you're already a dishonored man. You want to know how your men feel about you? They told me they felt fooled by you. Your task now is to regain your honor and make them respect you again. Otherwise how can you command the squad?"

Kong lowered his eyes without a word. I was impressed by Deng's pointed speech, to which I couldn't add anything. By nature, Deng was a reticent man. Obviously this matter had been preying on his mind for a while, though we had talked of it only twice. I felt bad, because I was the company's political instructor and Party secretary and I should have done something about the affair before the election.

After Kong left, I admitted my negligence to Deng and promised that I would try every means to stop the affair. Deng was always forthright and said we should have taken action when I showed him those candy wrappers three weeks before.

The next morning I sent Scribe Yang to Garlic Village to investigate the girl. I told him to go to the production brigade's Party branch first, look through her file, and find out all the information about her and her family background. "Trust me, Instructor Pan," Yang said with a smile. "I'm a professional sleuth." He swung a thin leg over a Forever bicycle and rode away with the handle bell tinkling.

Then I set about writing a report on our preliminary election to the Regimental Political Department. I had graduated from middle school, so the writing wasn't difficult, and I finished it in an hour. Having nothing else to do before lunch, I considered Kong's case again, particularly the girl involved. I remembered she had a pleasant voice. On National Day the year before, we had heard her singing an aria from the revolutionary model play *Seaport* at the marketplace. She worked in the village's tofu plant, where our cooks would go to buy dried bean curd and soy sprouts. Though tall and delicate, she wasn't pretty, and there were freckles on her cheeks. She often reminded me of a giant fox in human clothes. Among all the girls at the Youth Home, I would say she was the least attractive.

The scribe returned at noon. I was shocked by the results of his investigation:

An Mali, 23, female
Family Background: Capitalist
Personal Class Status: Student
Political Aspect: Mass

An Long (An Mali's father), male, died in 2
Class Status: Capitalist; owned two textile mills before
    Liberation
Political Aspect: Counterrevolutionary

The true nature of the affair was clear now. If he knew her family background, Kong must have lost his senses and ignored the class distinction. As a high school graduate, he must have read too many Russian novels, in particular Turgenev, whom I had once heard him praise beyond measure, as though the story-maker were as great as Lenin and Stalin. Kong acted like a petty intellectual, who believed in romances and universal love.

After exchanging views on the new discovery, Deng and I decided to talk to Kong again. The next afternoon, when the other soldiers were wearing straw hats and hoeing potatoes on the mountain, Kong sat in the headquarters answering our questions.

"Did you talk to An Mali?" I said.

"Not yet."

"When do you plan to do it?" Deng put in.

"Probably this weekend."

"Comrade Kong Kai," I said, "do you know what her family background is?"

He nodded.

"Then why do you fool around with that capitalist's daughter?" Deng asked.

"She's not a capitalist, is she?"

"What? You don't mind having a counterrevolutionary capitalist as your father-in-law?" Deng thumped the desk.

"Commander Deng, Mali's father died years ago. She's an orphan now and I'll have no in-laws. Besides, she was born and raised under the Red Flag like me."

"You, you — "

"Kong Kai," I broke in, since Deng was not his match in this sort of verbal skirmish, "your offense is twofold. First, you violated the rule that allows no soldier to have an affair; second, you crossed the class line. Chairman Mao has instructed us: There is no love without a reason, and there is no hatred without a reason; the proletariat has the proletarian love, whereas the bourgeoisie has the bourgeois love. As a Communist Party member, to which class do you belong?"

Kong hung his head in silence. Deng launched an attack again. "What can you say now?"

No answer.

"You're ill, Little Kong," Deng went on in a voice full of comradely affection. "Everybody gets ill sometimes, but you shouldn't hide your illness for fear of being cured."

"Today we called you in," I added, "because we care about you and your future. We want to remind you of the dangerous nature of the affair."

Seeing that he seemed too ashamed to talk, I thought it better to dismiss him, so I said, "We don't need to talk more about this. You understand it well and must decide how to quit it yourself, the sooner the better. If you don't have anything to say, you're free to go."

Slowly he stood up and dragged himself out, with his cap in his hand.

"You should've ordered him to quit it," Deng said to me. I was surprised and didn't say anything. He went on, "He's so stubborn. How can we let him lead the squad? It's all right to fall into a pit, but he simply refuses to get out. How — "

"Old Deng, let's give him some time. He promised to quit it."

As I expected, Kong entered the larch woods with the girl on Sunday. This was necessary, because he needed to meet her once more to break it off; I didn't ask him to report progress. I wouldn't give him the wrong impression that I enjoyed seeing young people suffer. As long as he quit in time, it would be fine with me.

I met Kong several times the next week. Judging from his calm appearance, it seemed he had disentangled himself. But the following Sunday, Scribe Yang, who had been assigned to keep an eye on him, reported that Kong had sneaked out. I told him to go look for Kong in the larch woods and bring him to my office immediately, together with the girl. An hour later, Yang returned empty-handed and said they were not in the woods. Then I sent him, with the orderly, to search the village. They spotted the lovers, who were lying in each other's arms on the sandy bank of a stream, under a wooden bridge, but the couple slunk away at the sight of the searchers. Yang and Zhu returned with a used condom as evidence.

I was worried and dispatched the orderly to the Fifth Squad to wait for Kong and bring him over the moment he returned.

Kong arrived at my office two hours later. He said he had talked to her, but it didn't help. "How come?" I asked.

"She cried her heart out. I can't bear to hurt her. Besides . . ."

"Besides what?"

"I've promised to marry her."

"What? That's out of the question. You must stop it."

"Instructor Pan, Mali isn't a bad girl. She loves the Party and Chairman Mao. You can go ask the commune members."

"I don't want to judge whether she is good or bad. You're a Party member and must not marry a capitalist's daughter. Do you understand?"

"Please help me, my instructor!"

"I am helping you, to get out of this mess." I lost my temper, though I was well known for being patient.

"No, I can't hurt her. It's too much for me."

"All right, let me lay bare everything here. You must make your choice between that girl and your future. If you choose her, you'll be expelled from the army."

"Damn," he cried. "I can't decide."

"Then let me help. Tell me, can you give up your party membership for her?"

He stared at me in silence and seemed overwhelmed by the dark picture. I continued, "What would your parents say if they were here? Would they allow you to take a capitalist's daughter as your bride?"

"No, they wouldn't."

"Right, because it would bring shame to your family. Tell me again, don't you want to be an exemplary soldier and send home a red certificate?"

He didn't answer. I asked again. "Don't you want to be an officer someday and command troops?"

I took his silence as acquiescence. "See, you've been light-headed these days and never thought of the price you'll have to pay. No man in his right mind should ruin his future this way. I don't mean you shouldn't have love. We are all human beings and have emotions, but there are things more important, beyond love. A lot of revolutionary martyrs sacrificed their lives for the Party and the New China. Didn't they have love? Of course they did. They loved our nation and the revolutionary cause more than themselves. Now you are merely asked to quit an abnormal affair, but you say you can't. How can the Party trust you?"

He remained silent. I felt my talk had struck him hard and was boosting his determination, so I ordered, "Write her a letter and say it's over." To comfort him some, I added, "Little Kong, it's not worth it to make such a sacrifice for a girl. A real man must never put a woman before his career. I tell you this not as a Party secretary but as an experienced elder brother. Believe me, someday you'll marry a girl better than An Mali in every way. For the time being, it may hurt, but you'll get over it soon."

"All right," he muttered, "I'll write her a letter."

"Good. After you finish it, bring it over. I'll have it delivered to her. This may make you feel better."

At dinner I told Commander Deng about the talk and assured him that this was final. He also thought it was wise to resort to writing and having the letter delivered for Kong, because that would prevent him from seeing the girl again. In the evening the letter arrived, and we were surprised by its ludicrous brevity. Deng complained, saying we had to make Kong write another one, but I felt this would do, short as it was. The letter read:

June 12

Mali,

Please forget me. I love you, but we belong to different classes. There is no way for us to be together. I will not see you anymore. Take care.

Kai

With my fountain pen I deleted the words "I love you, but," so that the writing became pithier. Meanwhile, I couldn't help wondering why Kong hadn't written a full page. He was one of our best writers. Very often he read out his long articles at lunch to the entire company, showing off his verbal command. A typical petty intellectual.

Immediately we dispatched Orderly Zhu to the Youth Home with the letter. An hour later he returned and reported that the girl had burst out wailing when she read it. Good, it struck home, we all agreed.

I was awakened by Commander Deng around three the next morning. He said Kong Kai was gone. I jumped out of bed, and together we went to the Fifth Squad. At first we were afraid he might have defected to Russia, but after seeing his uniforms and submachine gun, we felt that was unlikely. No one would defect empty-handed; besides, the Wusuli River was high now and Kong was a poor swimmer. Yet we sent out the Second Platoon to the river searching for him. Then Commander Deng, Scribe Yang, and I hurried along to Garlic Village, believing Kong was more likely to be at the Youth Home. But on the way we ran into a band of militia, who said they were looking for An Mali, who had disappeared after reading the letter. This information scared us, because we thought the lovers might have committed suicide. We returned immediately, woke up the other three platoons, and began combing the nearby fields, woods, ponds, and cliffs. The soldiers never stopped cursing Kong while searching.

Many villagers joined us in the search, which continued for a whole day, but there was no trace of the couple. The Regimental Headquarters was somehow convinced that they were alive and had eloped, so it sent out a message to all the police stations in the nearby counties and cities, demanding to have them detained. That had never occurred to us. Who would imagine two bedbugs could jump to the clouds! Now the nature of the affair changed entirely, and they became criminals at large. If they were caught, Kong would be court-martialed and An Mali would become a current counterrevolutionary. "I'll blow that bastard to pieces if I get hold of him," Deng kept saying. For two days we were at a loss about how to deal with the situation; there had been no precedent in our battalion.

We believed they would be caught within a month or two, because there seemed to be no place for them to hide. Wherever they went, they would be illegal residents and easily identified by the police and the revolutionary masses. However, China was such a large country that you couldn't deny there might be a village or a small town where they could settle down. Our regiment sent people to Shanghai and Kong's hometown in Jiangsu Province, but the couple had never shown up at either place. Three months passed; still there was no news of their whereabouts. To punish me and Deng for our negligence, the Regimental Political Department gave us each a disciplinary warning. Deng was mad at me, because he believed I hadn't taken strong measures in time to stop Kong and should have borne the responsibility alone. There was bad feeling between us for at least a year.

The next summer I received a letter two days before Army Day. It had no return address, though the postmark revealed it was from Gansu Province. It contained only a photo, black and white and three by four inches in size, in which Kong Kai and An Mali sat together with a fat baby on their knees. Kong looked silly, but obviously healthy and happy; his hair stuck out like a magpie's nest. His bride smirked a little to someone beyond the camera. They looked like peasants now, and both had put on some weight. The background was blurred, perhaps deliberately, and there seemed a hillock behind them. In the upper left corner hung these words: "A

Joyful Family." After spitting on their faces, I turned the picture over and found a big word in pencil: "Sorry." I couldn't stop cursing them to myself. My first impulse was to send the photo to the Regimental Political Department, but on second thought I changed my mind, not because I didn't want to have them caught but because I couldn't afford to stir up more bad feeling between Deng and me. In addition, our superiors might reconsider my involvement in the case, suspecting Kong had maintained a correspondence with me. No, to send the photo on would be to set fire to my own house. So I struck a match and burned it, together with the envelope.

Uncle Piao's Birthday Dinners

It was December 28 by the lunar calendar. Squad Leader Han Feng and I brought back our lunch, sorghum and stewed tofu, and put it on the floor of the guest room in Uncle Piao's house, where the five of us from the Sixth Squad were quartered. Before we could take out the bowls and spoons, the door of the family room opened, and Uncle Piao's large white head appeared behind the frame. He waved his hand, summoning us. "Today's my birthday. Come and eat with me." He spoke Chinese with a thick Korean accent.

We looked at each other and didn't know if we should obey him. "Thank you, Uncle Piao, but we have our own lunch here," Squad Leader Han said.

"Come on, all of you." The old man gesticulated forcefully, the corners of his pouchy eyes wrinkling up.

Getting up from the floor, we had no idea how to deal with the invitation. It was said that the Koreans were so sincere that they would be offended if you didn't act like their close friends in their homes. Guanmen Village had about three dozen Korean families. They all kept their own customs and lived in convex-roofed houses, in which the floor and the bed were the same.

In the middle of the family room stood a short-legged dining table. Beside it was a basin of rice sending up warm steam in the sunlight. A large bowl of hot soy-paste soup occupied the center of the table, on which there were several dishes and pieces of tableware — kimchee, jellied pork, miniature dumplings, a liquor pot with six small porcelain cups, and six pairs of chopsticks upon six deep plates. Mrs. Piao and their youngest daughter, Shunji, knelt near the two large caldrons set into the floor in a corner; they were ready to serve us. We didn't know what to do. The old man had not told us a word about his birthday beforehand.

"Sit down," Uncle Piao said. "All of you. Come close, close to the table." He pulled my arm. "Sit here, Little Fan."

We all sat down. I tried hard to sit cross-legged in the Korean manner, but my legs were as stiff as wood. Except Squad Leader Han, the rest of us — Hsiao Bing, Jia Min, Jin Hsin, and I — couldn't bend our feet backward far enough to sit that way. The squad leader unbuttoned his collar.

"Eat and drink," Uncle Piao said, picking up a pair of chopsticks. His wife and daughter moved close with wooden ladles in their hands.

"Just a minute, please." Squad Leader Han stopped them. The two women lowered their eyes and knelt beside me. "Uncle Piao," Han said, "thank you for inviting us, but we cannot eat your food. We cannot break the rule, you know."

"What rule?" the old man stopped pouring liquor into a cup; the skin around his big nose crinkled. On his right cheek, the purple mole seemed to grow larger.

"The Second Rule: Do not take a needle or a piece of thread from the people. That's Chairman Mao's instruction," Han said.

"That's true," Jia Min and I said in unison.

"Drop it! Don't give me so many rules in my own home. I make rules here. I want you boys to eat. You don't take anything from me."

"You know, Uncle Piao, we will violate the discipline and be punished if we eat with you without the company leaders' permission." Han smiled as he kept shooting glances at the dishes on the table.

My mouth was watering. We had not tasted meat for a month, and every one of us might have dared to take a bite of a live pig. It was too much to have these good things in front of you when you could not touch them. "Uncle Piao," Jin Hsin said, "please let us go!"

"Today is my sixtieth birthday. I've invited all of you as my friends, but you don't want to show your faces at my table. You shame me!" The old man's nostrils were expanding, and he was red to the neck. Mrs. Piao said something in Korean that sounded like an admonition not to shout.

Bang. Uncle Piao struck the table with the chopsticks. His wife lowered her head. The brown soup was rippling in the pottery bowl. "All right, if you boys don't eat I won't celebrate this birthday, no more!" He leapt to his feet.

"Please listen to me," our squad leader begged, but it was no use. The old man pushed the door open and began throwing the food together with the containers into the yard. The soup bowl flew through the air, leaving behind a brown line on the white ground, landed beside a pear tree, and disappeared in the snow. Pieces of pickled cabbages, pork cubes, and dumplings were scattered everywhere in the yard. A flock of chickens and a few crows arrived at once and began eating away. Their heads were bobbing up and down. It was windless outside, and the sun was shining in the blue sky.

Mrs. Piao held the basin of rice and moved it behind her. Shunji was sobbing. Uncle Piao put on his boots and went out without his fur hat.

We all lost our wits. The squad leader ran out to look for Uncle Piao, while the four of us retreated to our room and ate our own lunch. He did not get hold of the old man, who drove his bullock cart north to transport coal. There were a lot of coal pits in the mountain, and Squad Leader Han didn't know which one was Uncle Piao's. Han returned spiritless. Since neither Mrs. Piao nor their daughter understood Chinese, it was impossible for us to explain to them.

That evening our company's Party secretary, Wang Hsi, and Commander Meng Yun came to the Piaos to apologize. The family had just finished dinner. We gathered in the guest room, watching them through the narrow opening of the door. They were all sitting on the floor, and Uncle Piao was himself again and looked quite happy. After taking away the bowls and dishes, Mrs. Piao placed three small cups of kimchee juice on the dining table. To our surprise, the leaders thanked the old man and both emptied the cups in one gulp.

"Good, that's an army man, Ha-ha," Uncle Piao said.

"Uncle," Secretary Wang said, "we came to apologize for what happened at noon. Our men spoiled your birthday dinner. Please forgive us."

"No, no, it's my fault. I had a bad temper." The old man looked a little embarrassed, and he turned to his wife, who smiled with her palm covering her mouth.

"Uncle Piao, we promise you that won't happen again," Commander Meng said.

"It's all over now. Please don't mention it again." The old man drank the last drop of the juice. "To tell you the truth, we Koreans like only straightforward men. I know these boys are good, but they behave like timid girls in my home. You see, they're soldiers, carrying guns and firing cannons; they should be more spunky. Korean women are crazy about spunky men."

We couldn't help tittering behind the door. They all turned to us and then laughed heartily. His daughter Shunji was not present, and Mrs. Piao didn't seem to understand what her husband had said.

"Uncle Piao," Secretary Wang said, "we'll celebrate your birthday the day after tomorrow."

"It's on our company," Commander Meng added. "We'll bring wine and dishes. All right?"

"All right. Ha-ha, wonderful! I love Chinese food more than Chinese women." The old man's eyes flashed a bit in the dim light. They shook hands and got up from the floor.

The company leaders came into our room and told us that from now on if a Korean gave us something, we must not refuse. First we should accept it and then find a way to pay him back. In any case, we must not impair the friendship between the people and the army.

Two days later the whole company had the Spring Festival feast. The mess squad cooked six dishes — stewed boar meat with potato noodles, fried ribbonfish, cabbage and bean jelly, scrambled eggs with mushrooms, pork and tree ears, and turnip slivers mixed with sugar and vinegar, so we just brought back some extra of each dish for the Piaos. The cooks didn't do anything special for Uncle Piao's birthday dinner, but the mess officer gave us two large bottles of white spirits, one of which was for the old man.

Mrs. Piao took out a dozen plates, and every one of them was at once filled with our food. Their eldest daughter, Shunzhen, happened to come home with her two sons for a visit. All the men, including the small boys, ate at the large table, while all the women were at a small table. The Piaos also prepared something — a huge bowl of dumplings and, of course, a plate of kimchee. As soon as we'd set everything up, Commander Meng arrived. Then dinner started.

A kerosene lamp, hanging from the ceiling, shed coppery light on the yellow floor and the white walls. Everybody was free to serve himself, since there was no host today. Commander Meng raised his cup and proposed a toast: "Uncle Piao, to your health and longevity!"

"Happy birthday, Uncle Piao," we said almost simultaneously and clinked our cups with his.

"Everybody's happy," the old man said with his mouth full of food. He couldn't contain his happiness. Except for me and Jia Min, all the men, including the two small boys, drank up the liquor in one gulp. Immediately every cup was refilled.

The women ate away quietly; they smiled and murmured something in Korean. Obviously, they liked the food and maybe enjoyed not having to serve us. I stole a glance at Shunji. She must have drunk quite a bit, for her face was pink, and two dimples deepened below her plump cheeks. She was listening to her sister.

Mrs. Piao used a ladle to give us each some dumplings. I wanted to have more rice and covered up my bowl with my hand, so she gave my share to Jia Min, whose bowl already had some dumplings inside. "Have more," she said timidly in Chinese, smiling at Jia.

After a bite, Jia started to cough; he looked tearful. I couldn't tell why. Hsiao Bing wagged the tip of his tongue around his lips.

Commander Meng left after three cups, because he had to visit other families and attend the banquet held for the village powers in the production brigade's meeting room. Uncle Piao didn't press him to stay. In fact, we felt more relaxed once the officer had gone. Now we could eat and talk freely.

Soon Uncle Piao's tongue loosened. He told us stories about the Japanese and the Russian troops, and even allowed us to touch the big scar on his crown inflicted by the Japanese police because he had carried a small bag of rice around his waist for his sick old mother.

"Only the Japanese could eat rice," he said. "The Koreans were allowed to eat only millet. For the Chinese, only sorghum and corn."

"How about soybeans?" I asked.

"No soybeans. The Japs burned soy and wheat to drive locomotives that carried all the minerals and lumber to the seaport. From there they shipped them back to Japan."

"They were beasts!" our squad leader said, his voice full of hatred.

"The Russians are no better," Uncle Piao went on. "The Big Noses and the Small Noses are all barbarians. In the fall of 1945, in Hutou Town, I saw with my own eyes a Russian officer rape a Chinese woman. He put a pistol on the threshold of the house and raped her inside. The husband and the other Chinese men stood outside and dared not go in, even though the woman was screaming for help. Once you're conquered by foreigners, you've lost everything. You don't have the right to be a man."

"But the Russians came to fight the Japanese, didn't they?" Hsiao Bing asked.

"That is true." Uncle Piao nodded. "But they were bandits. Most of them were in fact the Whites sent over by Stalin to fight the Japs as a punishment. They didn't care who their enemy was, they just killed people and enjoyed themselves."

"Like the Japs?" I asked.

"Sure, they'd kill anybody in their way. In Hutou at that time, there was a food vendor called Mu Shan, a Chinese acquaintance of mine. When the Russian troops marched into the town, he was selling ravioli by the roadside. A Russian soldier walked out of the procession, grabbed Mu's basket, took out some ravioli, and ate them. Then came the Russian Army Police, who wore red stripes. Mu complained to the police. Can you guess what those officers said?"

"What did they say?" Jia asked.

"They said they were going to open the Russian soldier's stomach. If there was ravioli inside, it was all right. If there was no ravioli inside, they would shoot Mu on the spot. Mu knelt down, begging them to forget it. Who would think a few ravioli worth a man's life! The police refused to listen. One officer grabbed a carbine and shot the man, who was trying to escape. They cut his stomach open and found the food in there. They raised their thumbs to us and said, 'Ho-lashao!' It means 'good' in Russian."

"They are Tartars," Jin Hsin said.

"Yes, they're beasts. That's why we welcome you to stay here, to fight the Russians and defend our homes and land."

We were moved by his last sentence. Raising our cups, we drank up the last drops. Mrs. Piao cleared away the cups and dishes, and she brought out a large teapot and some small bowls. We began drinking tea and eating peanuts. Uncle Piao summoned his daughters to dance for us. What an embarrassing idea. But the two sisters didn't hesitate at all and started wheeling before us so naturally. They enacted "The Korean People Love Great Leader Chairman Mao," a sort of Loyalty Dance. Their long silk skirts waved around while their mother clapped her small hands, crying, "Chaota! Chaota!" That means "wonderful" in Korean. The flame of the kerosene lamp was flickering with the women's movements. Their shadows were flowing on the floor and the walls as if the whole house was revolving.

When they finished, they bowed to us, and we all applauded. Shunji looked like a young bride in her loose, white dress.

Guzhe and Guhua, Uncle Piao's grandsons, began to set off firecrackers outside. I went out to join them. They dared not light the big ones, so I helped them. With a burning incense stick, I launched the double-bang crackers into the sky one by one. It was snowing lightly. The air smelled of gunpowder as clusters of explosions bloomed among the dim stars.

I heard somebody approaching from behind; before I could turn around, a heavy slap landed on my back. "Fan Hsiong, you son of an ass," Jia Min said out loud. "You didn't want the dumplings and had them put in my bowl. You're a smart fox. Oh, I had to eat them all before I could eat rice."

"What's wrong with you?"

"There's no meat in the dumplings, only chili and peanut oil. Damn you, they gave me a lot of blisters inside my mouth."

I laughed. Jia kicked my legs and wanted to whack me again. I fled, running around Uncle Piao's house. He chased me around and around until I hid myself in a haystack.

"Fan Fox, get out of your hole," Jia shouted. I kept quiet.

He searched about in the yard and around the house but couldn't find me. Meanwhile, the two small boys each held high a string of tiny firecrackers tied to a bamboo pole, and Jin Hsin lit both strings. At once the successive explosions joined the rumbling of the large battle of fireworks that was seething throughout the village. The hay smelled so fresh it reminded me of the Spring Festival's Eve when I had played hide-and-seek with my pals at home.

Shunji began singing in the house. From the window lattices covered by plastic film, Uncle Piao's and Squad Leader Han's laughter rose and fell, echoing in the cold night.

Love in the Air

After the political study, Chief Jiang turned on both the transmitter and the receiver and started searching for the station of the Regional Headquarters. Half a minute later a resonant signal emerged calling the Fifth Regiment. Kang Wandou, who had served for two years, could tell it was an experienced hand at the opposite end. The dots and dashes were clean and concrete; the pace was fast and steady.

"He's very good," Shi Wei said.

"Of course, Shenyang always has the best hands," Chief Jiang said, returning the call. This was their first direct communication with the Headquarters of Shenyang Military Region. In no time the two stations got in touch. Jiang telegraphed that from now on they would keep twenty-four-hour coverage.

"Understood. So long," Shenyang replied.

"So long," Jiang tapped. He turned off the transmitter, but left the receiver on. "Shun Min, it's your turn now. Little Kang will take over in the evening."

"All right." Shun moved his chair close to the machine.

Though the middle-aged chief called him Little Kang, to the other soldiers Kang was Big Kang. His whole person was marked by abnormal largeness except for his voice, which was small and soft. Whenever he spoke, he sounded as though he was mumbling to himself. If his neck were not so long, his comrades would have believed he had suffered from the "big-joint" disease in his childhood. His wrists were thick, and his square thumbs always embarrassed him. But everybody was impressed by the beautiful long lashes above his froggy eyes.

After dinner Kang replaced Shun. The evening shift was not busy. Since all news stations broadcast at dusk and there was too much noise in the air, few telegrams were dispatched or received during these hours. Kang's task was to answer Shenyang's call every hour, and for the rest of the time he had to attend to the receiver in case an emergency arose. Having nothing else to do, he opened the fanlight and watched the night. Gray streaks of clouds were floating rapidly beneath the crescent moon and the glimmering stars. In the air there was a mysterious humming, which seemed to come from the constellations. Except for the swarms of lights in Hutou Town, it was dark everywhere. Even the silhouette of those mountains in Russia had disappeared.

Cold wind kept gushing into the office; Kang closed the fanlight and sat back on the chair. Again, nothing could be seen through the window, on whose frosty panes stretched miniature bushes, hills, caves, coral reefs. He picked up a pencil, turned over a telegram pad, and began drawing pictures. He drew a horse, a cow, a dog, a pig, a rooster, a lamb, a donkey, and a hen leading a flock of chicks.

After taps at nine, the quiet grew intolerable. If only he could have something interesting to do. In one of the drawers there was a volume of Chairman Mao's selected works and a copy of Lenin's *What Is to Be Done?*, which Chief Jiang would browse through at night, but these books were too profound for Kang. He missed the picture stories he had read when he was a boy. Those children's books could no longer be found anywhere, because they had been burned at the beginning of the Cultural Revolution. Kang took out his tobacco pouch and rolled a cigarette. Smoking was the only way to prevent himself from dozing off. Then he stretched his legs, rested his feet on the table, and leaned against the back of the chair as if lounging on a sofa. Soon the small office turned foggy.

Shenyang began to call at ten sharp. Kang turned on the transmitter and was ready to reply. It was another radio operator at the other end now. The signal was fluctuating at a much faster speed, approximately 130 numerals a minute. Because of the noise, the dots and the dashes didn't sound very clear, though they were distinguishable.

"Please answer," it ended.

Immediately Kang started to call back. His large hand held the button of the sending key and pounded out the letters one after another. He was a slow hand and could tap only eighty numerals a minute. But his fingers and thumb were powerful — whenever he telegraphed, the key with its heavy steel base would move about on the table. Holding the base with his left hand, he was repeating the reply signal in a resolute manner. His thick wrist was moving up and down while a little red light was flashing nervously at the top of the transmitter.

The operator at the opposite end did not hear Kang and resumed calling. Now there was less noise in the air and the signal became distinct. The call sign, composed of eight letters, was repeated again and again; it formed a crisp tune, flowing around and around. Kang pricked up his ears. This must be the chief of the station. He had never met such an excellent hand. There were automatic machines that could produce 180 numerals a minute clearly, but those dead instruments always sounded monotonous. They didn't have a character. The more you listened to them at night, the more likely you would fall asleep. But this fellow was one of those "machine defeaters."

"Please answer," the other side asked again.

Once more Kang went about calling back. Affected by the dexterous hand at the other end, he tried hard to speed up. The chair under his hips creaked while he was struggling with the bakelite key button, which turned slippery in his sweating hand.

Unfortunately this was a bad night. The other side simply could not find him. It called him time and again; Kang replied continually, but they could not get in touch. Forty minutes passed to no avail. By now, the other operator had become impatient. The melodious signal gradually lost its rhythm and flowed so rapidly that the letters were almost indistinguishable. It sounded like raindrops pattering on metal tiles. Patient as he was, Kang began to worry.

Around eleven, the telephone suddenly rang. Kang picked up the receiver and said, "Hello."

"Hello," a tingling female voice said. "This is the Military Region Station. Wake up, comrade. Have you heard me on the machine?"

"Ye-yes." Kang paused with surprise, his heart kicking and his throat tightening. Who could imagine a woman would call you on the border at night? "I-I've heard you," he managed to say. "I ne-never dozed off. I've been calling you all the time."

"Sorry, don't take it to heart. I was teasing you. Shall we switch to the second set of frequencies?" She sounded so pleasant.

"All righ-t." His tongue seemed not his own.

"Bye-bye now, meet you on the machine."

"Bye."

She hung up. Kang was dazed, still holding the receiver.

The sweet voice went on echoing in his ears, "Sorry, don't take it to heart. . . ."

The call sign appeared again. This time it repossessed its elegance and fluency, but to Kang every dot and dash was different now, as though they were tender, meaningful words the young woman sent to him alone.

"Switch frequency please," she ended.

Kang jerked his head and rushed to look for her on the new frequency. Without much effort, he found her again. His body grew tense as he became engrossed in the sways and ripples of the heavenly melody. How wonderful to work with a woman at night. If only she could call him like this for an hour. But she stopped and asked, "Please answer."

Kang's hand began to tremble. It settled on the sending key like a small turtle, shaking out every letter brokenly. He cursed his hand, "Come on, you coward! This is not a battle yet." He wiped his wet forehead with a telegram sheet.

What a pity. She heard him in less than a minute and replied promptly: "No business. Meet you at twelve o'clock. So long."

"So long." Kang had to agree, because it was a rule that an operator must never transmit an unnecessary dot or dash. The longer you stayed on the air, the easier it was for the Russians to locate your position.

Kang felt at a loss. He raised his head to look at the clock on the wall — eleven-ten, so he would meet her in fifty minutes. His imagination began to take wing. What was her name? How stupid he was, having forgotten to ask her. How old was she? She sounded so young and must have been around twenty. A good person, no doubt; that pleasant voice was full of good nature. What did she look like? Was she beautiful? Well educated? Intelligent? That voice told everything — all the best a woman could have. But what did she look like exactly? Tall and slim, with large black eyes? Of course he could not find out much about her through only one meeting. It had to take time. He believed that eventually he would get to know her well, because from now on they would meet every night.

The clock moved slowly, as though intending to avoid an ominous ending. Kang kept watching it and longed to arrive at the midnight rendezvous in the twinkling of an eye.

Suddenly somebody knocked at the door. Chief Jiang came in. "You can go to bed now, Kang. I happened to wake up a few minutes earlier tonight." He yawned.

Kang stood up and didn't know what to say. He tried to smile, but the effort distorted his face.

"What happened?" the chief asked. "You look as awake as a lynx."

"Nothing, everything is fine." Kang picked up his fur hat; with enormous dismay he slouched out. He forgot to take an apple, which was his night snack.

How could he sleep? Every inch of his skin was affected by a caressing tingle he had never experienced before. At the other side of the room, Shun was snoring and Shi murmured something in his dream.

"I was teasing you. . . ." The voice spoke to Kang again and again. He shut his eyes tight; he shook his head many times in order to get rid of her and go to sleep, but it was no use. She was so close to him, as if sitting right beside his bed in the dark, whispering and smiling.

Little by little, he gave up and allowed her to play whatever tricks she wanted to. The most unbearable mystery was what she looked like. He tried to think of all the women he knew, but he could not recall a pretty one. Surely he had aunts and cousins, surely he remembered some girls who had hoed the cornfields and cut millet together with him, but none of them differed much from his male relatives or from the men in his home village. Every one worked like a beast of burden, and none could speak without swearing.

The prettiest women he had ever seen were those female characters in the movie copies of the Revolutionary Model Plays, but most of them were too old, well beyond forty. How about the girl raped by the landlord in *The White-Haired Girl?* Yes, she was a wonderful ballerina, slim and good-looking. How deft her toes were. They capered around as if never touching the ground. She could swing her legs up well beyond her head. And the slender waist, which was full of rebellious spirit. What a wonderful body she had! But did she have a wonderful voice? No one could tell, because she kept quiet in the ballet.

No, she wouldn't do. He would not accept a woman who might lack that charming voice. Besides, that actress had long white hair like an old crone's. She must have been weird, or her hair wouldn't be so silvery.

How about the revolutionary's daughter in *The Story of the Red Lamp?* Well, that was a good one. But did she not seem too young? She was seventeen, old enough to be somebody's wife. A marriageable girl indeed. What he liked most about her was that long glossy braid, which reached her buttocks. But she was too thin and must have been too feeble to work. Her aquiline nose was narrow; that was not a sign of good fortune. Even worse, her voice was sharp. It was all right for singing Peking Opera to a large audience, but who dared to quarrel with a girl like that? In real life, she must have been a "small hot pepper." No, he had to look for another woman.

Now he had it — the female gymnastic athlete he had seen in a documentary film. She performed on the uneven bars. Her body was so supple and powerful that she could stretch, fly, and even somersault in the air. No doubt, that was a healthy energetic woman, not a bourgeois young lady who would fall in a gust of wind. What did she look like? He had not seen her face clearly in the film and could not tell. Then this woman had to go too, at least for the time being.

The radiator pipes started clinking and whistling gently. The boiler room pumped steam at four. With dawn approaching, Kang was worried and tried to force himself to sleep. But that voice would not leave him alone. "Wake up, comrade. Have you heard me on the machine? . . ." It sounded even more pleasant and more intimate. You fool, he cursed himself. How stupid you are — bewitched by an unknown voice! Forget it and get some sleep.

Soon he entered another world. He married a young woman who was also a telegrapher. They worked together at the post office in his hometown. They lived in a small house surrounded by a stone wall that had a gate with iron bars. Their garden was filled with vegetables and fruits. The beans were as broad as sickles, and the peaches as fat as babies' faces. Poultry were everywhere, three dozen chickens, twenty ducks, and eight geese. Who was his bride? He didn't know, for he only saw her back, a tall, sturdy young woman with a thick braid.

At breakfast he felt giddy. He could not tell if he had slept at all. Neither was he sure whether the prosperous domestic scene was his dream or his fantasy. How absurd the whole thing was. He had never loved a woman before, but all of a sudden he'd fallen in love with a voice. His first love was an unknown voice. He was scared, because he could not determine whether it was real love or merely a delusion from mental illness. Did people feel this way when they were in love? He felt sick and beside himself. How long would it take for him to grow used to this thing or get over it?

He could not sleep that morning when he was supposed to have a good rest to make up for the previous night and prepare himself for the evening shift. That voice, mixed with the call sign, whispered in his ears constantly. Time and again, he forced himself to think of something else, but he could not summon up anything interesting. He dared not smoke, for fear that Chief Jiang, who slept in the same room, would know he had remained awake for the whole morning.

In the afternoon, during the study of Chairman Mao's "Combat Liberalism," Kang was restless, longing for the arrival of the evening. The words grew blurred before his eyes. When he was asked to read out a page, he managed to accomplish the task with a whistling in his nose. His comrades looked at him strangely. When he finished, Shun said, "Kang, you must have a bad cold."

"Yes, it's a bad one." Kang blew his nose with a piece of newspaper. He was both miserable and hopeful. Probably the more he worked with her, the better he would feel. Everything was difficult in the beginning; the end of suffering was happiness. At the moment he must be patient; a few hours later, he would be in a different world.

How ruthless Heaven was. She did not show up in the evening. It was a different operator at the other end. Kang spent the six hours racking his brains about what kind of schedule she had. The following three evenings passed in the same fruitless way. Kang was baffled. Every night he could not help thinking of that mysterious woman — all women — for several hours. In the daytime he was very quiet. Although pining away, he dared not talk to anyone about it. How shameful it would be — to have it known that you were enchanted by a woman about whom you didn't know anything. How silly he was! That woman must have forgotten him like used water. No, she had never bothered about knowing him. How could she, a pretty young woman in the big city and perhaps surrounded by many smart officers in the headquarters, be interested in a soldier like him, who was so dull, so homely, and so rustic? He knew he was the toad that dreamed of eating a swan, but he couldn't help himself.

On Saturday morning, Kang was roused from his catnap by Shi Wei. "Big Kang, come and help your younger brother."

"What's up?"

"Too many telegrams this morning. I've been copying for three hours and can't handle it anymore."

"All right, I'm coming." It was almost eleven o'clock anyway. Kang got up and wiped his face with a wet towel.

There she was! He had hardly entered the office when Kang froze stock-still. The pleasant signal, for which he had been yearning for days, was singing proudly as though to a large audience. The dots and dashes sounded like amorous messages inviting him to decode their secret meanings. How magnificent her telegraphic style was in broad daylight. Kang lost himself in an imaginary melody composed of both the electric signal and the tingling voice — "Hello, this is the Military Region Station. Wake up, comrade. Have you heard me on the machine? . . ."

"What's the matter with you?" Shi rapped him on the shoulder.

"Oh nothing," Kang muttered, moving to the desk. "Never met such a good hand."

"True, he has gold fingers."

There was no time to tell Shi that it was she, not he, because the receiver was announcing: "Please ready."

Kang started writing down the numerals rapidly. In the beginning it went well, but soon his attention began to wander. He was distracted by his desire to appreciate the rhythm and the personal touch in the sounds, and he had to drop some numerals now and then. More awful, that voice jumped in to trouble him — "Sorry, don't take it to heart. I was teasing you. . . ."

"Repeat?" she asked, having finished the short telegram.

"Yes, noise," Kang pounded nervously. "Group eight in line four, from group three to eight in line six . . ."

Meanwhile, Shi Wei watched him closely. He was surprised to find Kang, a better transcriber than himself, unable to jot down the telegram sent out so clearly. There was no noise at all; why did he tap "noise" as an excuse? Kang was aware of Shi's observing and was sweating all over. He rushed to bring the receiving operation to an end.

"Are you all right?" Shi asked, after Kang signed his name on the telegram.

"I don't know." He felt sick. He got up and hurried out of the office.

Another fruitless evening and another sleepless night. Kang could no longer contain himself. On Sunday evening, he revealed the truth to Shi and Shun, who happened to be in the office.

"Shi Wei, you know, the Shenyang opreator with 'gold fingers' is a woman, not a man." He had planned to say a lot, to make a story, but he was bewildered, finding that he completed the project in just one sentence. He blushed to the ears with a strange emotion.

"Really?" Shi asked loudly. "No kidding? Why didn't you tell me earlier, Brother Kang?"

Kang smiled. Shun was not sure who they were talking about. "Which one?"

"The best one," Shi said with a thrill in his voice. "I can't believe it. A girl can telegraph so well. Tell me, Big Kang, how did you get to know her?"

"She called me, because she couldn't hear me," he declared proudly.

"What's her name?" Shi asked.

"I have no idea. Wish I knew."

40

"Must be a good girl. I'll go to Shenyang and get her."

"Come on, don't brag," Shun said. "I want to see how you can get her."

"You wait and see."

Kang was shocked that Shi was also interested in her. He regretted telling them the truth. If Shi made a move, Kang would have to give ground. Shi was an excellent basketball player and had in his wallet the pictures of a half dozen young women, who he claimed were all his girlfriends. In addition, his father was a divisional commissar in the navy; Shi had grown up in big cities and knew the world. Most important of all, he spent money like water. How could Kang compete against such a smart, handsome fellow?

It was this new development that made him fidgety that evening. He paced up and down in the office, chain-smoking for two hours. Finally, he decided to investigate who she was. He picked up the telephone and called the Shenyang Miliary Region. It took half an hour for the call to get through.

"Hello, this is Shenyang, can I help you?" an operator asked sleepily.

"Ye-yes," he struggled to say. "I want to speak to — to the wireless station, the one that communicates with Hutou?"

"What's 'Hutou'? A unit's code name?"

"No, it's a county."

"Oh, I see. Please tell me the number of the station you want to speak to."

"I don't know the number."

"I can't help you then. We have hundreds of stations, and they are in different cities and mountains. You have to tell me the number. Find the number first, then call back. All right?"

"Uh, all right."

"Bye-bye now."

"Bye."

It was so easy to run into a dead end. All the clever questions, which he had prepared to ask the radio operator on duty about that woman, had vanished from his mind. How foolish he was — having never thought there could be more than ten stations in the Regional Headquarters. What was to be done now? Without an address, he could not write to her; even with an address, he didn't know how to compose a love letter. Why was Heaven so merciless? It seemed that the only way to meet her was through the air, but he had not figured out her capricious schedule yet.

It did not make much difference after they rotated the shifts. Now Kang worked afternoons. No matter how exhausted he was when he went to bed at night, he would lie awake for a few hours thinking of one woman after another. His dreams ran wilder. Every night the pillow, which contained his underclothes, moved from beneath his head, little by little, into his arms. He was tormented by endless questions. What was it like to kiss and touch a woman? Did women also have hair on their bodies? Was he a normal man? And could he satisfy a woman? Was he not a neurotic, drenched in sweat and burning away like this in the dark? Could he have children with a woman?

Whenever he woke up from his broken sleep that mysterious voice would greet him, "Wake up, comrade. Have you heard me on the machine? . . ." The sounds grew deeper and deeper into him, as though they were sent out by his own internal organs. During these frantic nights, he discovered that Chief Jiang had to rouse Shi Wei at least three times every night. Shi worked the small hours.

Kang's skull felt numb in the daytime. He was convinced that he was a lunatic. How panicked he was when receiving a telegram, because that melodious signal and that tender voice, again and again, intruded themselves into his brain and forced him to pause in the middle of the transcribing. How good it would be to have peace once more. But peace of mind seemed remote, as though it belonged only to a time that he had outgrown and could never return to. Even the exercises in the mornings became a torture. He used to be able to write down 160 numerals per minute with ease, but now he had to struggle with 110. When they sat together reading documents and newspapers, his comrades often waved their hands before his eyes to test if he could see anything. Somebody would say, "Big Kang, why do you look like you lost your soul?" Another, "What do you see in your trance? A goddess?"

On these occasions Kang would let out a sigh. He dared not tell anybody about the ridculous "affair." He was afraid that he would be criticized for having contracted bourgeois liberalism or become a laughingstock.

One morning during the exercises, the telegraphic instructor, Han Jie, looked at Kang's transcription and said under his breath, "No wonder the Confidential Office complained."

Suddenly it dawned on Kang that he had become a nuisance in the Wireless Platoon. A pang seized his heart. No doubt, the confidential officers in the Regimental Headquarters were dissatisfied with his work and had reported him to the company's leaders. It was this stupid "affair" that had reduced him to such a state. He had to find a way to stop it — forget that woman and her bewitching voice — otherwise how could he survive? Although in his heart he knew he had to get rid of her, he didn't know how. Neither did he want to try.

On Thursday evening two weeks later, Chief Jiang held an urgent meeting at the station. Nobody knew what it was about. Kang was scared because he thought it might be about him. The secret would come out sooner or later. Had he babbled it during his sleep at night? He regretted drawing three pictures of women on the back of a telegram pad. Chief Jiang must have seen them. What should he say if the chief questioned him about those drawings?

The meeting had nothing to do with him. When Jiang asked Shi Wei to confess what he had done in the small hours, Kang at last felt relaxed. But like Shun, he was baffled about what had happened. Shi protested that he had not done anything wrong.

"You're dishonest, Comrade Shi Wei," the chief said.

"No, no Chief Jiang." Shi looked worried. "I did all the work well."

"You know our Party's policy: Leniency to those who confess, severity to those who refuse. It's up to yourself."

"Why?" Shi seemed puzzled. "This policy applies only to the class enemies. I'm your comrade, am I not?"

"Stop pretending you're innocent. Tell us the truth."

"No, I really didn't do anything wrong."

"All right, let me tell you what happened." The chief's voice grew sharper. "You were caught by the monitoring station. You thought you were smart. If you didn't want us to know, you shouldn't have done it in the first place. Look at the report yourself." He tossed the internal bulletin to Shi and handed Shun and Kang each a copy.

The title read: "Radio Operators Proffered Love in the Air." Kang's heart tightened. He turned a page and read "From February 3 on, from 1:00 A.M. to 5:00 A.M., a radio operator in the Fifth regiment and an operator at the 36th station of Shenyang Military Region have developed a love affair in the air. . . ."

Kang was stunned, and his thick lips parted. He could never imagine Shi would make such an unlawful move. A small part of their love talk was transcribed in the report:

I am Shi Wei. Your name?
Lili. Where are you from?
Dalian. And you?
Beijing.
Your age?
Twenty-one. And you?
Twenty-two. Love your hand.
Why?
It is good.
Why? Not love me?
Yes, I do.
!
Love me?
Maybe.
. . . . . .

Kang wanted to cry, but he controlled himself. He saw Shi's face turn pale and sweat break out on his smooth forehead. Meanwhile Shun bit his lower lip, trying hard not to laugh.

"Now, what do you want to say?" Jiang asked.

Shi lowered his eyes and remained silent. The chief announced that the Communication Company had decided to suspend Shi Wei from his work during the wait for the final punishment. From now on, Shi had to go to the study room during the day and write out his confession and self-criticism.

Though he was working two more hours a day to cover for Shi, Kang no longer expected to meet Lili, whose family name was not revealed in the bulletin. Obviously she was also suspended from her work and must have been doing the same thing as Shi did every day in the company's study room. But the tune created by her fingers and her charming voice were still with him; actually they hurt him more than before. He tried cursing her and imagining all the bad things that could be attributed to a woman in order to pull her out of himself. He thought of her as a "broken shoe" which was worn by everyone, a bitch that raised her tail to any male dog, a hag who was shunned by all decent men, a White Bone Demon living on innocent blood. Still, he could not get rid of her. Whenever he was receiving a telegram, her voice would break in to catch him. "Sorry, don't take it to heart. I was teasing you. . . ." It was miserable. The misery went so deep that when he spoke to his comrades he often heard himself moaning. He hated his own listless voice.

Shi's punishment was administered a week later. Both Shi Wei and Wang Lili were expelled from the army. This time the woman's full name was given. To Kang's surprise, Shi did not cry and seemed to take it with ease. He ate well and slept well, and went on smoking expensive cigarettes. Kang figured there must have been two reasons why Shi did not care. First, with the help of his father, he would have no problem finding a good job at home; second, the expulsion gave him an opportunity to continue his love affair with Wang Lili, since they were now two grasshoppers tied together by one thread. Lucky for Shi, he didn't lose his military status for nothing. It seemed he would go to Shenyang soon and have a happy time with her.

The station planned to hold a farewell party for Shi Wei. Though it was not an honorable discharge, they had worked with Shi for almost a year and had some good feelings about him. For days Kang had been thinking what souvenir he should give Shi Wei. He finally chose a pair of pillow towels, which cost him four *yuan*, half his monthly pay. In the meantime his scalp remained numb, and he still could not come to himself. Not only did the task of receiving a telegram frighten him, but any telegraphic signal would give him the creeps. He had developed another habit — cursing himself relentlessly for his daydreaming and for having allowed himself to degenerate into a walking corpse for that fickle woman, whose name he would now murmur many times every night.

Four older soldiers from the Wireless Platoon were invited to the farewell party. Chief Jiang presented an album to Shi, and Shun gave him a pair of nylon socks. When Kang's pillow towels were displayed, everybody burst out laughing, for on each towel was embroidered a pair of lovely mandarin ducks and a line of red characters. One said: "Happy Life," and the other: "Sweet Dreams." Peanut shells and pearstones fell on the floor because of the commotion the garish towels caused.

"You must be joking, Big Kang," Shi said, measuring one of the towels against his chest. "You think I'm going home to get married?"

"Why not?" Kang smiled. "Won't you go to Shenyang?"

"For what? I don't know anyone there."

Kang stood up. The floor seemed to be swaying beneath his feet. Tears welled up in his eyes. He picked up a mug and gulped the beer inside, his left hand holding the corner of the desk. He put down the mug, then turned to the door.

"Where are you going?" Chief Jiang asked.

Without replying, Kang went out into the open air. He wanted to bolt into the snow and run for hours, until his legs could no longer support him. But he paused. On the drill ground, a dozen soldiers from the Line Construction Platoon were practicing climbing telephone poles without wearing spikes. Behind the brick houses stood the thirty-meter-tall aerial, made of three poles connected to one another, which had been raised for their station by these fellow men. In the northeast, the Wusuli River displayed a series of green, steaming holes along its snow-covered course. On the fields and the slopes of the hills, a curtain of golden sparks, cast by the setting sun, was glittering. The gray forests stretched along the undulating mountain ridges toward the receding horizon. The sky was so high and the land so vast. Kang took a deep breath; a fresh contraction lingered in his chest. For the first time he felt a person was so small.

That evening he wrote a letter to the company's Party branch, imploring the leaders to transfer him to the Line Construction Platoon. He did not give an explicit reason, and merely said that somehow his mind was deteriorating and that he could not operate the telegraphic apparatus anymore. The letter ended as follows:

> If I can no longer serve the Revolutionary Cause and our Motherland with my brain, I can at least work with my hands, which are still young and strong. Please relieve me from the Wireless Platoon.

After writing the letter, he wept, filling his hands with tears. He used to believe that when he was demobilized he could make a decent living by working as a telegrapher at a post office or a train station, but now he had ruined his future. How painful it was to love and then give it up. If only he could forget that woman's voice and her telegraphic style. Whether he could or not, he had to try.

Dragon Head

I met Dragon Head on our first evening in Guanmen Village, which is twenty *li* north of Hutou. After the Battalion Headquarters settled in a small adobe house, whose owner of the landlord class had been exiled inland because of the tense situation at the border, the commander of the First Battery, Lin Hu, brought over a militiaman. They stepped in and whisked the snow off their clothes with their fur hats. The militiaman unbuttoned his blue overcoat, and a pair of large Mauser pistols, probably captured from the Japanese, were revealed at his flanks. He was tall and broad shouldered. The room grew darker as the flickering flame on the kerosene lamp cast his huge wavering shadow on the white wall.

"This is Militia Company Commander Long Yun," Lin Hu said. Then he turned to the militiaman. "This is our battalion commander, Gao Ping."

"How do you do?" I held out my hand.

"Happy to meet you," Long Yun said and put his mittens on the table. We shook hands. His palms and fingers felt like an emery wheel. "You can call me Dragon Head, Commander Gao. All my soldiers call me that, because my surname is Long — dragon, you know. Ha-ha-ha!" He laughed heartily, ruffling up his hair with his hand. Two rows of tea-stained square teeth were displayed under his straight nose and moistened mustache. His bulging black eyes glittered with the unrestrained candor that marks the men on the Northern Frontier. I smiled, amused by this young man who took the militia as the regular army.

"Commander Gao," Lin Hu said, "my battery has been lodged entirely, all together in seventeen homes. Our cannons and trucks are stationed at the threshing ground of the Third Production Team. If not for Dragon Head's help, some of us would have to sleep outside tonight and turn into frozen meat tomorrow morning."

"Don't be so polite, Commander Lin," Dragon Head said. "You fellas are the people's army, our own army. You came to defend our country and protect our homes and land. How can we let you sleep in the snow? Our houses are your houses, and our beds your beds too."

"Well said, Comrade Militiaman," Commissar Diao Shu said loudly as he came in from the next room. He stretched out his hand to Dragon Head and continued, "Chairman Mao instructs us: 'The army and his people have united as one man; see who can be our match under Heaven!'"

I moved forward a little, intending to introduce them, but Diao made a gesture to stop me. "We met two hours ago," he said to me, and then he turned to Dragon Head. "I'm glad to meet you again, Comrade Long. Ah, how could I forget 'Dragon Head'! What a thunderous name! From now on, we are friends and comrades-in-arms, am I right?"

"Right. We certainly are." Dragon Head looked pleased, his mouth spreading sideways with a broad smile. He inserted his hands behind the holsters of his pistols.

After they left, Commissar Diao and I went out to see how well the three batteries had been settled. He was to inspect the western half of the village; I would go through the eastern half. It was snowing lightly. A large flock of noisy crows flew by and merged into the indigo air. Stars, scrubbed by snowflakes, were dangling in the murky sky while kerosene lamps burst forth one after another at the windows of the dwarf houses. A whiff of fresh corn cake mingled with the smell of cow dung.

There were some two hundred and thirty homes in Guanmen Village, and our battalion, three hundred and four men, was quartered in ninety of them. We were a newly formed unit, whose three batteries came from three different armies in Liaoning Province. With brand-new weapons and equipment we arrived at the frontier to reinforce the anti-tank firepower of the Fifth Regiment. It looked like a war was about to break out. We were prepared to fight the Russians, and every one of the soldiers had written an oath in his own blood to show his determination to defend the Motherland. Before coming to Hutou, I had sent a letter home, telling Guihua, my wife, that she should marry another man if I could not return, but that she must take good care of our two children. The soldiers never complained about the hardship we had to undergo — no barracks, not enough nutritious food, the severe cold of Siberia. As the head of the battalion, it was my duty to make sure that every one of them had a warm place to sleep for the night. That evening I ended up having dinner with the Fifth Squad of the Third Battery at the eastern end of the village. We ate sorghum and stewed frozen radishes.

To express our gratitude to the villagers, we had a movie shown the following evening. People assembled at the marketplace in the center of the village, waiting excitedly to see *The Guerrillas on the Railroad*. A small electric generator was whining away, and two bulbs were shining on the poles holding the white screen. Pulling on long pipes, old men and old women sat on small stools, muffled up in fur overcoats. Young mothers held babies wrapped in cotton quilts, and the large gauze masks that shielded the women's noses and mouths exuded warm breath. Children were running around and through the crowds; some of them perched on naked trees, waiting for the movie to start.

As soon as our three batteries sat down, Dragon Head's men arrived. They were singing "Carry the Revolutionary Guns" and marching in good order directly to the front ground below the screen. All together about seventy of them passed by, and every one shouldered a weapon — Russian 1938 rifles, American carbines seized from Chiang Kai-shek's troops, three light machine guns of Japanese make, a small sixty-millimeter mortar also captured from the Japanese, a pair of antitank mines, and — most advanced of all — one Russian bazooka. A few soldiers rose to their knees to have a better view of the militia. Having noticed our attention, Dragon Head kept his men marching in place at the front for a good minute. Then he ordered loudly: "Si-t down!" In a unified hop they sat down on the ground. To my surprise, most of the militiamen, including Dragon Head, wore army uniforms, though without collar badges or hat insignia. It seemed they had really got it into their heads to emulate the regular army unit.

Hardly had they sat down than they started a song, "Down with the New Czar of Russian Revisionists." In their tuneless chanting, there was a deep, booming voice directing all other voices, as though dragging them to an uncertain end. I could tell it was Dragon Head.

When they finished, Dragon Head jumped up and shouted: "People's Army — "

"Sing us a song!" His men followed in one voice.

"People's Army — "

"Sing us a song!"

The Second Battery began to sing a song composed for Chairman Mao's quotation: "Who are our enemies? Who are our friends? This is a question of the first importance for the revolution. To ensure we will succeed in our revolution, we must unite with our real friends in order to attack our real enemies."

When our men finished singing, without a request from the army side, the militia started another song, which was also a quotation from Chairman Mao: "A revolution is not a dinner party, or writing an essay, or painting a picture, or doing embroidery; it cannot be so refined, so leisurely and gentle, so temperate, kind, courteous, restrained, and magnanimous. A revolution is an insurrection, an act of violence by which one class overthrows another." So they sang. But this time Dragon Head stood in front of his men, beating time with his big fists. The Mauser pistols were fluttering at his sides like a pair of hawks.

We had no time to sing another song back because the movie suddenly started. Soon, laughter and applause rose and fell in the hush of the night.

Both Commissar Diao and I were very busy. During the day he spent most of his time in the three batteries organizing the studies of Chairman Mao's works and the documents issued by the Central Committee, while I was engaged in training the soldiers to operate the cannons more efficiently in the severe weather. We had to be well practiced. Guanmen Village was fifteen *li* from the Wusuli River, and the Russians' tanks could cross the frozen river and arrive here within half an hour, so we had to be able to get ready in a very short time. My men were the best soldiers I had ever commanded; after three weeks' drill, we could go into battle in twenty minutes.

One morning after breakfast I was about to set out with my orderly, Liu Bing, for the Second Battery for a training inspection. Suddenly Ma Yibiao, the battery's commander, burst into the Battalion Headquarters. "Damn it, Commander Gao. Screw Dragon Head and his mother, damn it!" he shouted, panting hard.

"What's wrong, Old Ma?" I asked.

"Six of my men lost their hats!"

"Calm down, and explain it slowly. What exactly happened?" As I was speaking, Commissar Diao came in from the adjacent room.

"Early this morning, after the running exercises," Ma said, his face red, "some of my men went into the latrine to relieve themselves. Six of them were squatting there. Then a hooligan wearing a large gauze mask came in, picked up their hats one by one, and ran away."

"What?" I couldn't believe it. "Six men were robbed like that?"

"Yes, it's damned shameful. They thought it was a joke and merely shouted, 'A good man doesn't jump at a squatting man.' Once they realized it was serious business, it was too late and the hooligan had disappeared."

"Who's the robber, do you know?" I asked.

"It's a louse on a bald head — everybody can see it. He must be one of Dragon Head's men. Who else wants army hats?"

"I'm going to Dragon Head to question him."

"Wait a minute, Old Gao," Commissar Diao broke in. "Don't be hotheaded. We have to think about the whole thing before taking any action."

"Why is it so complex, Commissar Diao?" Ma asked.

"Because if we don't handle it well, it will damage our relationship with the villagers, which is vital for us now."

"Old Ma, I think Commissar Diao's right," I said. Then I turned to Diao and asked, "What do you think we should do?"

"I suggest we hold a meeting this evening. Discuss it first and see what we should do. For the time being, let's keep quiet about it."

We all agreed. Together with Ma Yibiao, I went to the Second Battery. On the drill ground made out of a small soccer field, the soldiers were practicing directed fire. In the line of six cannons, the third one stood under its canvas cover. Ma pointed at it and said, "See, four men in the Third Squad have no hats and cannot come outside in the cold, so this cannon is not operated."

I was enraged again and went directly to the Third Squad. In a small farmhouse, six bareheaded men were sitting on three benches, studying Chairman Mao's "On Protracted War." When they saw me come in, they bent their heads lower. I sat down and asked them what the robber looked like.

"We couldn't see his face, Commander Gao," said the squad leader, Li Lin. "He wore a pair of sunglasses and a gauze mask."

"How tall and how big is he?" I asked.

"About a hundred and seventy centimeters tall, I guess, and of slender build."

"I saw a wart under his left ear," said a short man, whose name I remembered was Ding Zhi.

"Yeah, I saw the wart too," another put in.

"You mean here?" Commander Ma asked, pointing his finger at the spot beneath his earlobe.

"Yes." They nodded.

"Damn his grandma, he's nobody but Wang Si, one of Dragon Head's bodyguards," Ma concluded.

"Good, we have clarified that," I said. "Did you write your names inside your hats?"

"No." They all shook their heads.

"Tell everybody to put his name inside his hat," I told Ma.

Not knowing what the next step should be, we left the squad and returned to the drill ground. I was not very satisfied with the Second Battery's training in directed fire, but I didn't say anything, because it took time to master the skills and we would mostly use point-blank shooting in fighting the Russians' tanks.

That evening all the battery commanders and political instructors gathered at Battalion Headquarters. Commissar Diao presided over the discussion. In the beginning, most of us suggested holding a formal talk with Dragon Head and requiring him to return the hats with a promise that this sort of thing would not happen again. But Commissar Diao disagreed. He argued, "Comrades, we have to think about this matter in connection with the overall situation. If you view it this way, six hats are nothing — "

"It's not a matter of hats," I interrupted him. "I would give him sixty if we had that many extras. Because of the loss of those hats, a squad can't go into action in such cold weather. Say an emergency arises now; a cannon will be automatically disabled. Isn't it absurd?"

"I fully understand your point, Old Gao," he said. "Wait till I finish, and see if I can make some sense." He turned to all the officers and continued, "We live in the villagers' homes, and you all know what kind of man Dragon Head is. In a way he's the head of the village. If we get on bad terms with him, we may turn the whole village against us. We came here to fight the Russians and have no time and energy to deal with Dragon Head. At this moment, the Russians are our enemy. Comrades, we have to learn how to unite with all forces that can be united to fight our chief enemy.

"Please think about our own situation again. In the Fifth Regiment we are the only new battalion and the only artillery unit; if a war breaks out, for sure we will have to play the major part in fighting the Russians' tanks. We are not afraid of that, since our cannons are designed to destroy them. But what if the Russian foot soldiers launch an attack at our batteries? Do you think the Regimental Headquarters will send over a company beforehand to protect us? I don't think so. You all know there is simply no infantry unit nearby. Do you think we ourselves have enough firepower to stop the Russian foot soldiers? I don't think so either. Dragon Head has a company; though not well equipped, it's the best available. As long as we're on good terms with him, the militia will fight for us. He likes fighting; all right, we bring his enthusiasm into play. It's true that the loss of six hats may disable a cannon for a while, but it's a small matter compared with the overall situation. I think even if we lose a squad permanently, still it's not as important as to have Dragon Head's company in our service. Now, everybody can say whatever he wants."

What could we say? Who could oppose such a balancing, calculating mind? We all agreed with him and were willing to drop this matter. I was very impressed by Commissar Diao's good sense and was full of respect for this small man.

Although we did not bicker with Dragon Head, still my bad feeling toward him would not die away easily. Bandits, I would say to myself. If this were the Old China, no doubt Dragon Head would become a small warlord. One day at noon I ran into him on the road in front of the village grocery. He walked dashingly, with two bodyguards following. I couldn't help staring at him, and he must have realized the resentment in my look. His eyes rolled toward me while his hand rose to his temple, saluting me in the mlitary manner. Instantly his guards saluted me too. I was forced to raise my hand in return. They passed by as if on patrol.

The Spring Festival was drawing near, and I was worried. All the three batteries were new, without any savings. How could we celebrate the holiday? Some soldiers would miss home, and their spirits would be low. How could we make them forget home and enjoy themselves, eating well and playing well? Surely we had to stay in combat readiness during the holiday period, but we also had to feast and make every man feel at ease in his own battery. The Regimental Logistics Department sent us four hundred *jin* of pork. Too little for three hundred men. What should we do? Both Commissar Diao and I were restless.

This time Dragon Head came to help us out. On the morning two days before the Spring Festival, a large group of militiamen arrived at our headquarters. In the front yard they were blowing *suona*, beating drums and gongs and letting off double-bang firecrackers. Commissar Diao and I rushed out. A broad red banner, with the golden words MILITIA OF GUANMEN on it, was flapping away in the north wind. Every one of them carried a gun on his back. Warm breath was puffing out from their mouths and nostrils. Dragon Head, standing at the front, raised his right hand while his left hand remained stuck behind his Mauser. Immediately the men moved to both sides and a pass was opened through them. Then ten pairs of men, poles on their shoulders, carried over ten boars, which were held upside down by hemp ropes tied to the hind trotters. They placed the frozen carcasses on the ground one by one in a line. The first boar was covered with a large piece of red paper on which a row of characters in black ink read: FOR OUR BELOVED LIBERATION ARMY.

I was moved and went to Dragon Head. We shook hands. Commissar Diao was also delighted; he held Dragon Head's hand and spoke. "We are very grateful, Comrade Dragon Head, and we won't forget the kindness and the trust of your people."

"It's our duty to bring our best wishes to our own army," Dragon Head said, wiping the frost off his mustache.

"Dragon Head," I said, "we won't take these free. We must pay you. Tell us how much for each."

"What?" He frowned. "Commander Gao, you're not treating us as your own people if you say so. All right, if you want to buy, we won't sell." He was about to turn to his men.

"Wait, wait," Commissar Diao intervened. "Commander Gao didn't mean to take you as outsiders, Dragon Head. Chairman Mao has instructed us not to take from the people 'a needle or a piece of thread.' You know, we must always follow the Chairman's instruction. Old Gao was not wrong to mention the price, but he forgot that these boars are not from common people but from another unit, from our comrade-in-arms Dragon Head's company. Please don't misunderstand us; we do want to accept your kind gifts."

"That's the way of saying things. Ha-ha-ha!" Dragon Head threw his head back and laughed. All his men followed him guffawing.

So we accepted the boars. Each company got three, and the Battalion Headquarters kept one. The major problem had been solved: as long as we had enough meat, it would not be difficult to feed our men.

At my suggestion, we planned to give a banquet to the village heads and the production brigade leaders on the Spring Fetival's Eve. We ought to find a way to pay them back for their kindness. For whatever reason, we should not take things from the people without giving them something in return. Those boars could by no means come from Dragon Head's own home. Besides, we had caused a great deal of inconvenience to the villagers ever since we began lodging in their homes. This was the time to show our gratitude. Commissar Diao supported the idea.

The banquet was held at the meeting room of the production brigade, which was cleaned up and decorated for this occasion. A pair of colorful lanterns hung at the entrance, and a couplet written on two broad bands of red paper was pasted on the walls on each side of the door: THE ARMY AND

THE PEOPLE ARE UNITED LIKE FISH AND WATER / WITH SOARING ASPIRATION WE WELCOME ANOTHER SPRING. I didn't think Scribe Niu Hsi had done a good job in making the poetry, but we were army men and shouldn't be fastidious about words. Inside the room twelve square tables were set in three lines, and at the center of each table four candles, as thick as grenades, stood burning. The room was ablaze with a swarm of flames.

On the army side, all the battery commanders and political instructors and the officers in the Battalion Headquarters attended; on the villagers' side, all the local powers were invited, including the head of the blacksmith's shop and the only doctor at the village clinic. All together there were about ninety people. The dishes were not fancy, but they were substantial: stewed pork, scrambled eggs, fried cutlass fish, horsemeat balls . . . Wine was plentiful — three full vats stood against the wall. After Commissar Diao and the Party secretary of the production brigade, Liu Ming, made their speeches, people started to enjoy themselves.

As the heads of the army, Diao and I were obligated to go to every table and to propose toasts, but Diao had little capacity for liquor, so we had arranged beforehand that I would carry out the obligation alone. Holding a green enamel mug, I made my way from table to table.

I met Dragon Head and his men at the eighth table, the noisiest one. They ate meatballs with their hands and had a large basket of cutlass fish in the middle of the other dishes. At the corner of the table lay a short braid of large garlic, which they had brought for the feast.

"Merry Spring Festival, Dragon Head," I said with a smile.

"Happy holiday, Commander Gao." He raised a huge bowl, which looked like a small basin, and took a gulp.

"Let us drink to our solidarity," I proposed.

"Sure, glasses dry." Seeing me hesitating, he said, "Why?

You don't want to? My bowl's three times bigger than your mug."

Without a word, I drank up the mugful of corn liquor and then held the mug upside down.

"Good man!" they cried in one voice.

Dragon Head raised the bowl to his mouth and started drinking. A purple vein was quivering on his neck. I watched him with admiration.

When he finished, one of his men said, "Brother Dragon can swallow a sea."

We shook hands, and his eyes shone with happiness. When I returned to my table, Commissar Diao awaited me there. We agreed that everything had gone well. He wanted to leave early to visit the men in the batteries. I told him that I wouldn't hang around for long and would go to the Third Battery soon. Apart from wishing the soldiers a happy Spring Festival, we would also make sure that everything was in good shape, because our battalion had been ordered to stay in first-degree combat readiness during the holiday. For a whole week everybody had to sleep with his clothes on.

The village's show team arrived and started performing in the front of the room. A man in light green silks and a woman in pink, both with painted faces, were wheeling around, singing in turn the local opera The Couple's Twirl. The woman sang:

> Watermelons here are big and sweet,
> We club roe deer in our backyard,
> Pheasants sneak in to steal wheat,
> Fish jump into pails and splash hard.
>
> But take me with you, my sweetheart,
> On your three-horse cart.
> We shall journey, never apart,
> Never apart, never apart . . .

I was about to leave, but Dragon Head came to my table with the large bowl in his hand. Behind him came Wang Si, carrying a plastic gasoline can containing white spirits. "Commander Gao," Dragon Head said, "I like . . . like your way of drinking. Let's have a-another." He held out his bowl and Wang Si filled it. A wart protruded beneath Wang Si's ear like a squashed fly.

"Dragon Head," I said, "you shouldn't drink more. We're in combat readiness now."

"This stuff won't hold us back." He drank up the whole bowl, then looked at me with his bloodred eyes. "We set out tonight . . . and drive . . . drive the Russian Tartars down . . . down into the Arctic Ocean. Give us orders, Com-Commander Gao."

"Dragon Head, you need a rest."

"No." He held out his bowl again, and Wang Si refilled it. "All the northern land, from Sakhalin . . . to Mo-Mongolia, is ours. The Russians took it . . . from us. We must take it back! Screw their ancestors, they killed my . . . my gre-great-grandpa in Vladivostok. He was . . . doing business there — "

"You need some sleep, Dragon Head," I said. "Wang Si and you, Ma Ding, take him home and put him into bed."

"It's Spring Festival," he mumbled. "I'm happy, ha-ppy —" His men supported him away.

After having told Niu Hsi to take care of the banquet, I left for the Third Battery. It was snowing outside, and the wind had slacked off. Firecrackers sputtered here and there in the sky; the air was filled with the smell of gunpowder. Every chimney was puffing out sparking smoke. The merry cries of children were drifting about, reminding me of home. Guihua must be making dumplings now, and Hong and Tiger must be following the dancing processions in the streets. When the dinner's ready at midnight, they'll set a seat for me and place an extra pair of chopsticks on the table . . .

Later I heard that Dragon Head's great-grandfather had indeed died in Vladivostok. It was said that he had been a very handsome man, wearing a long, glossy braid. When the Russians took the city, they set about seizing women everywhere. Dragon Head's great-grandfather was captured because he looked so beautiful that the Russians mistook him for a woman. They brought him to their billet, but when they groped between his thighs, they felt something there, so they thrust a sword into his throat. This must have been the reason why Dragon Head would not live with the Russians under the same sky.

We had a good Spring Festival, and all the men felt refreshed. After the holiday period, we could sleep again in our underclothes. But we could not relax our vigilance, because it was still winter, the season when the Russians' armored vehicles could cross the frozen river. With the intention of maintaining our combat effectiveness, we decided to have an emergency muster on the last Wednesday night of February.

In fact, this was the first night action we had ever taken at Guanmen. At eleven o'clock sharp, Orderly Liu Bing blew the bugle in the sleeping village. All the battery leaders had been informed in advance, but they had to order their men to act as if a battle had broken out at the front. No light was allowed; everything had to be done in the dark, because the Russians could locate our position and shell us if they saw a light. In no time, the tranquil night was teeming with the noises of dogs, footsteps, horses, orders, and starting trucks. A few chimneys began spouting smoke — the cooks of each battery were heating water, with which the drivers would start the frozen vehicles. I set off for the bank of the Husha Brook, beyond the western end of the village, where we had planned to assemble the three batteries.

Not until half an hour later did all of the three batteries arrive. Without lights on, a few trucks were still nosing about like whales on the surface of a white ocean. The long barrels of the cannons all pointed to the northeastern sky. Some artillerymen even went about digging pits to set in the spades. "Stop digging!" I shouted at them. They didn't know this was just a drill.

The battery commanders all came over and reported to me and Commissar Diao. Although we both thought it was not too bad for the entire battalion to pull out in half an hour in such severe weather, neither Diao nor I was satisfied, because according to the requirement we should be able to complete the action in twenty-five minutes. I told the leaders to return to their batteries and lead their men back to the village. "Tomorrow we'll sum up our experiences and see if we can make it quicker," I said.

As I was speaking, Dragon Head and his men came running toward us. He came directly to me, bareheaded, puffing out warm breath and fanning himself with his hat. "All my men're here. Are we leaving for the front now?"

"No, these are exercises." I glanced at Commissar Diao, whose face fell.

"Exercises!" Dragon Head yelled, and he put his hands on the Mauser pistols. "Exercises at midnight? Why the hell didn't you inform me before? Damn you both!"

"Comrade Dragon Head," Commissar Diao said, "please do not misunderstand us. Night fighting is our army's tradition, you know that. We didn't notify you beforehand because we didn't want to disturb you. This is not a real action, and we just had the cannons pulled out. Please forgive us."

"Damn it, see what you've done." He turned in the direction of the village, his hand pointing at the glimmering sky above the waves of the thatched roofs. "See, every family lit a fire for cooking, and I've ordered them to send the food here." He raised his voice, shouting to the crowd of his men. "Hey, Ma Ding you run back to the village and tell them to stop, no more cooking, and no more killing sheep and pigs."

I felt awful. But it was not our fault. Even all of our platoon leaders had not been told of the muster in advance; why should we inform the militia? Dragon Head had made the mess himself; yet it would be senseless to blame him. "Dragon Head," I said, "we apologize. I mean it sincerely. Tomorrow I'll go with you to apologize to the people, home by home."

"Drop your apology. Who wants it! We take you fellas as our own army. Then you have your secret plans and make asses of us all. We've been wronged, you know. You treat us as outsiders."

"Comrade Dragon Head," Commissar Diao said loudly, "you're mistaken. I swear by my Communist Party membership that we always regard your company as our own troops. Your company is our infantry force, but you see tonight we have purely artillery exercises. Even so, we should indeed have notified you in advance. Please accept our sincere apology and pass it on to the villagers. I promise, from now on, we will let you know all our plans of action."

"You always speak well, Commissar." Dragon Head looked somewhat pacified. "All right, it's not a big thing. Nobody's lost his head yet. I'll talk to them and they'll understand. But no second time."

"You have my word," Diao assured him.

After Dragon Head led his men away, Diao turned to me and said, "It's negligence on our part."

"Why? I don't think so. The exercises are a military action; how come we have to tell him beforehand?"

"Old Gao, you forgot the action is also political. It could

damage the relationship between the army and the people if it's not done appropriately."

"I agree, my comrade commissar. Only because we live here, we have to share everything with him. Fine, it's all right with me. I must say, it's a pity that those sheep and pigs were not butchered for a holiday. Next time I'll order Dragon Head's company to make a forced night march to Hutou Town. See how he'll enjoy that." We both laughed.

Although I said that, we dared not have another emergency muster for the rest of the winter. It would be unwise to wake up the whole village at night without giving a genuine reason. Besides, if we had done it too often, the villagers would have got used to it; when a real emergency arose, they might have ignored it as exercises. So we wouldn't try again. Dragon Head had our promise that he would always be informed. All right, he could have our word, but there was no need for us to carry it out.

2

Spring came, and the Wusuli River thawed. The tension on the border eased up . Since the deep water could obstruct the Russians' armored vehicles, a large battle was unlikely. As soon as the weather allowed, we set about constructing our barracks, which were located on the slope of a hill three *li* west of Guanmen Village. Every day we busied ourselves felling pines for lumber, trucking bricks and cement from Hutou, leveling and digging the ground, and quarrying rocks. The whole battalion turned into a construction brigade. Our artillery skills were out of practice, and many soldiers went about without uniforms on all the time. But we had to have our own barracks, the sooner the better, for it was impossible to live with the villagers for long without a bicker or a row. Besides, it was difficult to impose discipline on army men who rubbed shoulders with civilians every day. My men were chosen fighters from three renowned armies, and certainly they would attract the attention of the womenfolk. Affairs were reported one after another. A young widow even sneaked into the brick bed shared by three soldiers in the First Battery. We had to move out of the village as soon as possible.

As it had been divided between us, I was in charge of constructing the barracks, whereas Commissar Diao organized all political studies and handled our dealings with the local people. I would leave at dawn for the building site and return at night, so for three months Dragon Head was almost out of my mind.

Then one summer morning Scribe Niu Hsi and I went to Wudao Commune Administration to hire some experienced masons. When we were coming out of the Leopard Mouth, a pass between two steep hills, we heard some gunshots. On our right, a group of militiamen stood at the edge of a graveyard, aiming their rifles and firing at the foot of the hill. Some of the shots whined away in the air and hit nothing. Dragon Head stood with arms akimbo. He saw us and waved. We got off our bicycles, laid them at the roadside, and went up to him.

"Hey, Commander Gao." He held out his hand. "Haven't seen you for a long time."

We shook hands and began to chat. He told me this was their practice range. There were two targets erected against a deserted quarry a hundred meters away. Numerous tiny white balloons, tied to the boles of young birches by threads, were fluttering in the warm breeze.

"It's a good idea to shoot balloons," I said. "A good way to practice how to shoot paratroops."

"You think so?" Dragon Head asked with a broad smile. "It's no fun to fire at dead objects, you know."

"Maybe we should use balloons in our practice too. Where did you get these?"

Dragon Head and the men around laughed. "It's easy, from the Commune's Family Planning Office. Free. Ha-ha-ha."

I shook my head and smiled. There was no way that we could get condoms free for our firing practice. At this moment, Wang Si, bareheaded, ran over and reported to Dragon Head, "Big Brother, everything's fixed now. We can start again."

Dragon Head turned to me and Niu Hsi. "Want to shoot down a paratrooper, eh?"

"All right," I said.

They gave each of us an old Russian rifle and five long cartridges. We loaded the guns and started to fire away. After every shot we pulled back the bolt lever to throw out the shell. Niu hit one "paratrooper," while I got four.

"Not bad, Commander Gao," Dragon Head said. "I can tell you're an old hand with guns. Not bad." Then he took a rifle from Ma Ding and fired rapidly at the floating targets. With five shots he brought down five.

"Good job!" I said. "Dragon Head, you're a marksman."

He narrowed one of his large eyes. "If I have a semiautomatic rifle like those used by your army, then I can wipe out all the paratroopers in seconds."

In fact, now only three were left bobbing in the distant air. A man holding a bunch of fully inflated condoms was about to leave to set up more. "Wait," Dragon Head ordered. "Wait a minute, Li Wu. We haven't done the real work yet." He turned to me and asked, "Don't you want to try the machine gun?" His hand pointed at a light machine gun of Japanese make that perched at the edge of a sunken grave.

I hesitated, because I had never touched a machine gun that old. "You know, Dragon Head, I'm not good at machine guns. I can handle any artillery pieces but not this kind of gun."

"Don't be modest," he said. "I know you're an old hand.

You shoot at the right target and leave the left one for me, okay? We'll do it just for fun."

Without my agreement, Ma Ding skillfully loaded the gun. "You have fifty rounds," Ma said in a nasal voice.

Somehow I did feel like giving it a try; so, lying prone at the side of the grave, I began shooting away. Clouds of dust were thrown up below and above the target as if I was raking the quarry. The recoil was so tremendous that the gun jerked and jolted in my arms like a struggling beast. A straight line of misty balls jumped up from the ground twenty meters ahead of me, stretching beyond to the top of the hill. The last few shots were sent into the faraway clouds.

"Damn it!" I shook my head, which was still ringing inside. "This gun fires like a machine cannon. I wasn't prepared for it." The men around were laughing.

Dragon Head smiled as though to himself and said, "I can tell you're not familiar with it. It's not so hard to handle once you're used to it."

In the meantime, Ma Ding loaded the gun with another fifty rounds. Dragon Head pulled the visor of his cap around to the back of his head, jumped into the grave, and started shooting at the target on the left. The gun was honking in fixed fire — every three or four cracks formed a beat. Wooden splinters flew about the green human silhouette, behind which bullets were whistling off rocks in all directions. The target quaked as if it would fall down. I could tell that most of the shots hit the mark. Wry smiles trembled on his face as Dragon Head fired away, until he split the target's wooden leg and swept the whole thing out of sight.

All the men shouted "Bravo." Li Wu ran off toward the quarry to count the hits. A black dog was dashing ahead of him.

"A great job, Dragon Head!" I said, stretching out my hand. "How did you learn to use guns?"

"Through hunting when I was a boy." He grinned at me. "But shotguns are no good, and we have sold all of them."

"How about these brothers?" I moved my hand around. "Do they also shoot so well?"

"No," Wang Si broke in, "only Brother Dragon can do it."

"Some of them are good gunmen, I must say," Dragon Head said.

"Hey," Li Wu shouted from the quarry, raising the fallen target, "forty-six hits."

"I wish they were forty-six Russian bastards," Dragon Head grunted.

Then, pointing at the standing target, Li Wu announced in a cry: "Se-ven."

All the militiamen laughed again. I felt embarrassed. It was the worst record in my life. If I had known the gun was so difficult to control, I would not have tried it or at least would have been more careful with it, and I wouldn't have made a fool of myself like this.

We had no interest in lingering any longer, so Scribe Niu Hsi and I left them for our bicycles on the roadside. I told Niu not to tell anyone in our battalion about the shooting, and he promised he would not. To be honest, I did not take the slightest offense at the experience, for Dragon Head was indeed a superior shooter. A superb marksman, I had to admit. Actually, nobody in my battalion could be his match. It was said that he could shoot eggs from fifty paces off with his Mausers in both hands. What made me so cautious was that I was the head of the army unit. If my men had known I participated in the militia's range practice, they would have followed me and started messing with those men.

By the end of August, we had finished the construction work. Four rows of brick houses were put up on the slope beyond the western hill. A small drill ground was flattened out halfway up the slope, where we would put our trucks and cannons. The major virtue of the barracks was that it was behind the hill, so the Russian lookout towers could not see us and their gunfire could not bombard us. Now the three batteries were busy packing up and pulling down all the temporary dining sheds, storehouses, and latrines that we had built in the village. For four months I had not taken one day off, so on a Saturday evening I accepted Commissar Diao's advice to have a break and go to Hutou the next morning, where I would take a hot bath in the town bathhouse and eat sautéed beef liver at a restaurant. Then I would pay a visit to an officer at the Regimental Headquarters who was from my hometown.

In Hutou everything went as I had planned. Around three o'clock, I walked back to the bus station at the town center, still a little hungover from the three bottles of brandy I had drunk with my fellow townsman. There I came across Dragon Head again; he was also waiting to take the bus home. With him was a familiar-looking girl.

"Hello, Dragon Head," I said. "Why are you here?" We shook hands.

"Went to Hsiufen's grandpa's home in Garlic Village." He pointed at the girl and introduced her. "This is my fiancée, Hsiufen."

"I'm happy to know you two are engaged. Congratulations." Then I said to the girl, "See how important you are? Dragon Head, the commander of the militia company, follows you around as your fully armed bodyguard." She smiled, and her clear, large eyes rolled toward her betrothed.

"Commander Gao," Dragon Head said, slapping his Mauser pistols. "I'm not carrying these fellows as presents for my in-laws, am I? Who knows when the Russians will come. We must keep them warm all the time." By "them" he meant the guns. The girl looked at me rather seriously and seemed to expect a positive response.

"You really have high vigilance," I managed to say. He smiled, and so did the girl. I felt awkward, because I didn't have my pistol with me. It was unnecessary to carry a gun when you were off duty in the summer. Truly, in the winter you could see many people bear weapons in the streets of Hutou; if you ate in a restaurant, very often some militiamen sat nearby, drinking and rejoicing, with their loaded guns propped against their tables. But other than in winter, few people carried weapons in town.

The bus arrived, and people were lining up to get aboard. I deliberately stood at the end of the line, not wanting to sit with Dragon Head and his fiancée, because I must have reeked of alcohol. As they moved slowly to the bus, I had a good look at the girl. She was tall, with a neck as white as that of a young goose. Her narrow nose pointed upward above a mouth shaped like a water chestnut. Her pink shirt and sky blue pants bulged a little around her breasts and hips. A pair of plastic sandals revealed her large feet. In a way, she seemed to match Dragon Head well in size and stature.

On the bus Dragon Head greeted a man behind him, then chatted with another man on his right. He appeared to know everybody. The conductor began to sell tickets. When she came to Dragon Head's seat, he handed her a one-*yuan* bill and said, "Two for Guanmen."

The driver in the front turned around and said aloud to the conductor, "Dragon Head doesn't need to pay."

"What?" Dragon Head said. "Don't try buying off a revolutionary, Old Zhao. I have to pay, because the bus is our country's. If you owned it, I'd take a ride directly to my brick bed at home." A few passengers laughed. The conductor accepted his money and gave him two tickets.

"Together with Hsiufen?" the driver asked, giggling without turning his head.

"Damn you, Monkey Zhao," Dragon Head retorted. His fiancée flushed a little and turned her head away. Some people chuckled, looking at the girl.

The bus pulled out. On the roadside, cement wire poles fell behind one by one, and bulletin boards, wider and taller than a soccer goal, moved past one after another. A white line of Chairman Mao's instructions paraded on a brick wall: DIG DEEP HOLES, STORE GRAIN EVERYWHERE, DO NOT LORD OVER THE WORLD! From the side I peered at the girl who sat beyond Dragon Head by the window. Against the breeze her curly bangs were fluttering on her smooth forehead. Her chin set forward a little, giving a clear contour to her face, while her eyes were half closed.

Somehow she felt me observing her. She turned around and gave me a childlike smile. All of a sudden I felt pity for her, not because of her beauty, which was in no way extraordinary, or because of my amorous attention, but because of the man she was engaged to. Dragon Head was not a bad fellow, but he was unreliable and could never be a good husband. Marrying a man of his kind is like building a home below a dam. I would have no child rather than allow my daughter to be such a man's wife.

The bus jolted to a stop at Guanmen Village. About a dozen passengers got off. Before I could wave good-bye to him and his fiancée, Dragon Head stopped me. "I want to have a chat with you, Commander Gao." Then he pointed to an aspen.

We moved a few steps to the tree, leaving the girl standing alone at the bus stop. "You can do me a favor, can't you, Commander Gao?"

"What favor?"

"We need a pair of transceivers."

"What for?"

"We often go to the Wusuli River to keep an eye on the Russians. But we can't go all together. You see, those of us on the river and those at home must find a way to keep in touch. I know you just got a bunch of new transceivers. Can you give us two of the big ones?" He was referring to some old three-watt transceivers that had just been put out of service.

"No, Dragon Head, I can't," I said firmly. "We do have some old ones, but they have all been listed and numbered, and we have to return them to the Regimental Logistics Department."

"Why do they want them back? They won't use them, will they?" He looked quite cross.

"I have no idea. According to the rule, we have to send back every one of the machines. Forgive me, Dragon Head. It's not personal. Say, if you wanted a transistor radio of mine, I would give it to you, but this is a matter of discipline."

"All right, I understand discipline all right. We won't ask you for them again." Without saying one more word, he turned around and walked away to the girl. His large shadow, cast by the setting sun, covered a long strip of land ahead of him.

That night Commissar Diao and I had a drink. I took out a packet of sliced pork head that I had brought from Hutou, and he told Orderly Liu to get a bottle of corn liquor from his room. "Old Gao," he said, "we two should really get loose tonight. Ha! Pork head, I haven't tasted this since we came here." He picked a chunk and put it into his mouth. "Hum, so good. Delicious!"

I smiled and poured the liquor into my green mug.

Two mugs later, I told him that I had met Dragon Head in

Hutou and that he had asked me for two transceivers. "Crazy. He's more vigilant than we are," I said.

"He's just that kind of man. You cannot do anything about it — it's easy to change a mountain or a river but not a man's nature."

"He's too warlike," I said. "It's the busy farming season now. Fields need hoeing and vegetables must be sown, but he and his men patrol around carrying guns and banners. It looks like he can't live without war."

"I agree with you, Old Gao, a hundred percent." Diao's tongue was a little thick. I didn't advise him to stop drinking; today we were off duty and should relax.

"I know his type well," he said again, and stuck a piece of the meat into his mouth. "What do you think would be his best end, O-Old Gao?"

"I've never thought about it. What do you think?"

"His best end is to be killed by our enemy." He chuckled. "I can see you're shocked, but I told you the truth. My granduncle was like that too, the same . . . same type." He raised his mug and drank.

"Same as Dragon Head?"

"Yes. My granduncle used to be a landlord, a ri-rich one. He overrode the entire village. Nobody dared oppose him, and he took care of everybody's business. For instance, a cart driver stole a chi-chicken from a farmer's house; he led the farmer to . . . to the cart driver's home, carrying a big stone, and they smashed the only caldron on the kitchen range. The family couldn't cook for many days. Everybody said my granduncle would be avenged sooner or later. My dad told me that he would have been e-executed by the Communists, if — if he had lived longer."

"How did he die?" I was curious. Diao would never talk like this when he was sober.

"How?" He giggled, shaking his head. "He was beheaded

by the Japanese devils. The Japs surrounded our village and brought all the folk to — to the marketplace. They ordered them to tell where the guerrillas hid themselves. The folk didn't know. The Japs set two straw cutters in the front of the crowd and said they would chop off some heads if the folk didn't tell them. My granduncle stepped out and said he knew, but he wouldn't tell. The Japs were mad and or-ordered him to go down on his knees. He refused. They beat him to the ground with gun butts, and . . . and put him under the blade. Still he wouldn't tell, and never stopped cursing, so they cut his head off."

"What happened then?"

"The villagers all said that only my granduncle knew . . . where the guerrillas were, and that he was the liaison man of the guerrillas. In fact he was not. Since he had been killed, the Japs let the folk go in the end."

"That's a heroic story," I said, a little moved.

"A funny one." He giggled again, but his eyes looked teary. He turned his face to the gloomy wall. After a few sec-onds, he resumed. "The truth is that all the folk hated his guts, but nobody dared touch him, because he was the lo-lord in the village. If the Japs had not killed him, the folk would have buried him alive when the Communists came to start the Land Reform. Beheaded by the Japs, he became a hero, a famous one. People in the nearby counties would men-mention his name as a true Chinese. All the villagers were grateful and thought . . . he had sacrificed himself to save their lives. He didn't love them a bit, to say nothing of sacrificing his life for them. I don't think the idea of sacrifice had ever entered his head. Who knows what the devil was in him . . . that drove him to step out. The funniest part is that — when the Land Reform was about to begin, the head of the Work Group told my grandpa, in secret, to sell all our land. Promptly my grandpa sold it and told everybody . . .

that my granduncle had left a large debt, and that we had to sell everything to clear the debt. So when the reform began, the villagers voted the Diaos' class status to be middle peasant, since we were indeed as lan-landless as any of them. Isn't it funny that the richest landlord turned into a middle peasant overnight?"

He giggled huskily. "You see, if my granduncle had been alive, we would've been classified as a landlord family. The folk would never have let us Diaos go. They would have wiped us out. If so, I couldn't be here, commanding the Communist troops."

"Old Diao, you cannot deny that your granduncle's deed is a revolutionary part in your family history." Although I said that, I felt his family's class status should have remained as landlord.

"Humph, what's history?" He emptied his mug, giggling again. The tiny flame on the kerosene lamp flickered on the table. "History is a mess of chances and accidents. It's true that my granduncle was killed by the Japs for his own good, for the villagers' good, and for our family's good. But while lying be-beneath the blade of the cutter, he couldn't know the meaning of his death, could he? It's all the later occurrences that made his death meaningful, isn't it?"

"You may be right, I'm not sure." I was somehow puzzled by his way of thinking. "Then how do you compare your granduncle and Dragon Head?"

"Old Gao, you're really a simple, honest man. My granduncle died in the hands of our national enemy. That's why we Diaos are still a Revolutionary Martyr's Family. Likewise, if Dragon Head is killed by the Russians, or by anyone who happens to be our enemy, he'll be a hero. Don't you think so?"

"I've never thought of it that way," I admitted. "I don't like Dragon Head much, but I can't tell how he'll end. He's so young, probably not thirty yet. Maybe he'll live longer than I. Who knows?"

"How humorous!" He laughed, his round eyes shining a little in the dim light. "I didn't know you had a sense of humor, Old Gao. Let's forget Dragon Head. Cheers."

We drank the last drop. He returned to his room. I went to mine, leaving the mugs and the chopsticks on the table for the orderly to clear away.

At four o'clock the next morning, I was woken up by a call from the Third Battery. Commander Meng spoke on the phone. "Our storehouse was broken into."

"What's lost?"

"I don't know exactly at this moment. Commander Gao, I'm leaving for the storehouse now, and I will inform you immediately after I know."

"I'm coming. See you at the storehouse." I put on my clothes and pistol and set out for the western end of the village.

The dawn was just breaking, and it felt rather chilly walking through the moist air. Five minutes later, I was at the storehouse, where Commander Meng, Political Instructor Wang Hsin, and two soldiers on sentry duty had already gathered. There was a hole, as large as a jeep wheel, in the back wall. "Commander Gao, two of the transceivers are missing, so far as we can tell," Meng reported.

"Fortunately," Instructor Wang said, "our ammunition has been moved to the new barracks — "

"Son of a rabbit," I cut him short. "It's Dragon Head! Yesterday afternoon he asked me for transceivers. I refused him, so he had them stolen at night. I'll go and question him."

"No, you should not." Commissar Diao emerged from behind. "Old Gao, don't act rashly. We have to think about this."

At this moment a clatter of horses' hooves came from the east. We all turned to watch. A group of fully armed militia riders were ambling away from the village. Their broad red standard was waving slightly in the pink dawn. One rider was carrying a dark box on his back. No doubt it was a transceiver. Dragon Head rode at the front on a large black horse, leading them northward to the Wusuli River.

"Damn them all," I cursed. "I hope they'll be put out of action by the Russians."

"Old Gao, calm down, please," the commissar said. "We'll get him sooner or later. One cannot eat up a fat man in one bite." Then he turned to the others. "You can all go back now. Commander Gao and I will handle this by ourselves. No one else is to know of this."

After they left, the commissar and I made our way back to the Battalion Headquarters. I couldn't help cursing, but Diao remained quiet.

"I'll grab hold of him this evening and recover those machines," I assured Diao.

"Don't do it. Please listen to me, Old Gao. It's not time yet to settle things with him. Don't you remember the saying that goes: 'Today you caper about swaying your butt, tomorrow we'll rip out your guts'?"

"I know that, but if we don't stop him now, tomorrow he'll steal our trucks and cannons." We turned at the corner of the village millhouse.

"No, they don't know how to drive a truck. They are horsemen." He looked somewhat mysterious. "To tell you the truth, Dragon Head is on the list, and he will be dealt with eventually."

"What list?" I stopped.

"I don't know exactly. Anyway, we two cannot handle him. He's too big for us. As a matter of fact, I have to call Regimental Commissar Feng Zhi and report on the whole thing. We shouldn't do anything before hearing from the Regimental Political Department."

This was entirely new to me. I had never thought Dragon Head was so important that some secret eyes kept him under surveillance. That morning Diao called the regimental commissar and was told to wait for a decision.

The order came after lunch. When Scribe Niu Hsi was cutting my hair in the middle of the yard, Commissar Diao came in and told me, "Old Gao, I just received a call from Commissar Feng. He told us to be quiet, as if nothing had happened."

"All right, I'll be as quiet as a deaf-mute," I said, keeping my head low for Niu Hsi to shave the hair on my nape. I felt Diao looked rather unnatural, perhaps because of what he had divulged to me the night before.

"I've got your word, Old Gao. So the case's dropped now." He was about to leave.

"Hold on," I called him, and he turned back. "Old Diao, from now on, I don't want to have anything to do with Dragon Head. I cannot endure him, and I may wind up calling him names and making a scene. So please deal with him yourself."

"That's not a bad idea — I mean, to avoid clashes. He's not so difficult to persuade. Fine, from now on I'll stroke the dragon's whiskers."

A week later, we all moved into our new barracks, and for the rest of the year I didn't see Dragon Head again. It seemed that I had indeed washed my hands of whatever he did.

3

Because the Chinese and Russian governments had started to negotiate, the situation at the border was much less intense than it had been the previous year. Except for three days' combat readiness in early March, it was rather peaceful throughout the winter. We spent most of the time carrying out drills and criticizing Lin Biao, who had plotted to assassinate Chairman Mao. It seemed the Russians had changed their minds and would not invade our country anymore. Over seventy of our older soldiers were demobilized in January. By now we had completely dissolved our contact with Dragon Head and his men. Even Commissar Diao no longer believed that we might need the militia as foot soldiers to defend our cannon emplacement.

When spring arrived, I gave orders that each battery must open up wasteland as much as it could and sow soybeans and vegetables. That was the way to improve our food quality. Soybeans were vital, for out of them you can make oil, tofu, and soy milk. The next step was to raise pigs; every battery had to get thirty piglets. I told the soldiers, "Now we must learn not only how to fight but also how to live."

Dragon Head had not changed a bit. His men would still ride to the Wusuli River to keep watch on the Russians. Very often, when hoeing in the fields, we could hear gunshots — they never stopped practicing. Because we lived in our own barracks, we had no dealings with them. I ordered my men not to be mixed up with the militia without my or Commissar Diao's permission.

One summer afternoon we were planting cabbages near our barracks. As I was fetching water from a ditch with a pair of buckets, an explosion thundered in the north. Then some shells landed randomly, and numerous dark smoke pillars rose in the woods and in the fields. Large fireballs bounced along on the plain. One shell whistled by over our heads and exploded two hundred meters away in a valley. This is war. The Russians are bombarding us. I dropped the buckets and ran back to the barracks.

Orderly Liu blew the bugle, and all our men dashed to the

cannons. But I had no idea what orders I should give next. I called the Regimental Headquarters, and they didn't know what was going on either. "What am I supposed to do? Wait to be shelled in the barracks?" I yelled at the staff officer on the phone.

"Old Gao" — Regimental Commander Zhang Yi spoke now — "it's not war. Remain where you are. We'll know the truth soon." The phone was hung up.

Carrying my binoculars, I scrambled to the top of the hill to have a view of the northern land. There they were. Through the glasses I saw Dragon Head and his men, about twenty of them, riding desperately back along a path through the birch woods. Two Russian gunboats on the river were firing at our side aimlessly. To my surprise, another boat, full of smoke, was motionless, and its crew were leaving it. They jumped into the water, swimming to the other boats.

"Damn it, it's Dragon Head's men," I told Commissar Diao, who had just come up, gasping for breath.

"Let me have a look." He took the binoculars from me and watched.

"It seems that the militia had a skirmish with the Russians on the river," I said.

"A gunboat is sinking, but I can't see the militia."

"Let me have a look again." I got the binoculars and watched. Now the disabled boat had disappeared, while the other two were retreating to their base. The gunfire had stopped. Everything had returned to normal.

Half an hour after we came back to the barracks, Dragon Head and his cavalry arrived. Commissar Diao and I went out to meet them. All the horses were sweating, and some of the militiamen stood by their horses, bareheaded. Dragon Head couldn't help laughing. "Record a merit for us, Commander Gao and Commissar Diao," he shouted. "We got rid of one of the Russians' river rats."

"Who gave you the orders to do it?" I asked.

"We did it ourselves. What an experience. Bang, just one bazooka shot, and it crept no more. We lost nothing but some caps."

"You should not have done it, Dragon Head," I said loudly, "The surface of the river is a neutral zone. This may cause a war."

"War? Sure, we're fighting a war with the Russians, aren't we? That's why you're here." He looked irritated. "Tell me, Commander Gao, which side are you on?"

"Cool it, Comrade Dragon Head." Commissar Diao intervened. "I will report the victory to the Regimental Headquarters. I assure you that the Party and the people will not forget this heroic deed. Now you fellows return home and have a good rest. We will inform you of the merit soon."

"On your horses!" Dragon Head ordered. They all leapt into their saddles. "Commissar Diao, I'll wait for your word," he said from the back of his black horse.

"Sure, you wait," Diao returned in a low voice.

They all dashed off, leaving behind a dusty cloud. I turned to Diao and asked, "Why did you call it a victory?"

"Don't be angry, Old Gao. Is a name so important?"

"I don't know how to play on words, Comrade Commissar. Neither do I bear a grudge against Dragon Head personally. He's a brave fellow, I agree. But this is a matter of principle — we must never fire the first shot."

"I won't argue with you, because what you said is absolutely right. But we had to find a way to dismiss him, didn't we?"

I didn't answer, although I had to admit to myself that he was not wrong. We went separately to the batteries to explain to the leaders what had happened.

The final decision arrived two weeks later. No merit citation was awarded to Dragon Head, but his militia company received an internal commendation which said: "Let the Invaders Come but Not Return." I was bewildered. Why should the higher-ups praise the militiamen? Did they intend to encourage them to provoke the Russians again? Then why did we have to obey the orders not to fire the first shot? When I raised these doubts with Diao, he smiled and said, "You wait and see. It's not over yet."

As he predicted, a month later the Military Department of Hutou County issued an order that required all the militiamen to turn their weapons over to the Military Department. From now on, private possession of these weapons would be dealt with as a crime. Because every piece of arms had been listed and numbered, each militiaman had no choice but to hand in whatever happened to be in his hands. Even a dagger or an ammunition belt had to go. At once, Dragon Head's company was disarmed.

"In a way, I feel sorry for them," I told Commissar Diao one day. "They have had guns for quite a few years, then suddenly everything is gone."

"You have a good heart, Old Gao," Diao said, laughing.

I laughed too. "It must feel like you had a tidy sum in the bank yesterday, then overnight you're penniless." Although I said this, I did believe it had to be done that way. It was not safe to have so many civilians armed with guns when the Russians didn't seem eager to attack anymore.

The disarmament delivered a considerable blow to Dragon Head. A month later I ran into him in Guanmen Village, where I had my leather shoes repaired. I stood at the door of the cobbler's shop, watching with amusement a group of kids forcing a bear cub to climb to the top of a flagpole that rose in the middle of the village square. "Up, up," they shouted. Two long bamboo poles were poking the young animal from beneath. A boy catapulted a pebble at the rump of the bear, which at once sprang up two meters.

Here came Dragon Head. He walked alone, his feet kicking away horse droppings now and then. His head drooped forward, as though he were watching his own shadow. The front of his gray jacket was open, revealing a large red character "Loyalty" on his white undershirt. He saw me standing by and turned his head away. His right hand moved unconsciously to his flank, which one of the Mausers used to occupy.

"Dragon Head, how are you doing?" I walked up to him, holding out my hand.

"Not bad, still alive," he muttered. We shook hands. His large face was expressionless, and his eyes were ringed with yellow.

I felt somewhat uneasy and managed to ask, "When will I drink your wedding wine? You're going to get married soon, aren't you?"

"Not soon." He shook his head. "Maybe at the Spring Festival. I don't know."

"Don't forget to invite me, and we'll have a few."

"Sure, I'll have you over." He smiled, his large eyes glittering a little.

"Anything I can do for you, please let me know, all right?"

"Sure. Thank you for saying that, Commander Gao."

Although I had said that, I had no idea how I could help him. In fact, I could not, because what he really needed was nothing but weapons, without which he could not be the former Dragon Head again. Since the disarmament, the militia company had been literally disbanded. Now Dragon Head's men would be carrying hoes and spades to the fields instead of riding with arms to the river.

Fall came. We were busy getting in crops, felling trees for fuel, and digging vegetable cellars. For a month the three batteries had not taken the canvas covers off their cannons.

Everybody worked hard; even the cooks could not go to bed until midnight, because they had to pickle a lot of vegetables — cabbages, turnips, eggplants, green peppers, garlic, and the like. By the end of September, we had finished most of the preparations for the winter. Now we could spare some men and sent them to help the villagers in Guanmen with their harvest and their threshing and winnowing.

On the evening of October 1, National Day, right after the holiday feast, the leader of the mess squad, Mu Lin, burst into the Battalion Headquarters. At the sight of Diao and me, he cried, "Our guns are stolen!"

"What?" I jumped to my feet. "What guns? How many?"

"Two semiautomatic rifles," he said, panting hard. "They just disappeared this afternoon, when we were busy cooking the dinner."

"Damn it, it must be Dragon Head again. Let's go." I put on my pistol and went out with Mu. Commissar Diao and Scribe Niu came along with us, but they didn't wear their pistols.

No trace of the crime could be found at the mess squad. Two guns, which the cooks had seen on the rack at noon, were missing. No doubt it was the work of Dragon Head's men. But without any evidence in our hands, what could we do? I couldn't help swearing.

"Commander Gao," Scribe Niu interrupted me, "I saw Ma Ding fooling around in the bushes this afternoon. He must have pretended to cut firewood there."

I turned to Diao. "We must send a squad to Guanmen and bring Ma Ding here."

"Why the hurry?" Diao asked.

"This time it's not transceivers but guns, my commissar."

"They won't shoot us with the stolen guns, will they?" Without waiting for my answer, he continued, "Let them keep the guns warm in their hands for a little while. It won't hurt us. Dragon Head has done enough now, and he won't get away with it this time. I'm going to report this to the Regimental Political Department. For sure, they will start an investigation immediately."

What he said made sense, for Dragon Head was not our enemy and would never fire at us. There was no point in acting rashly. Besides, we did not have any evidence yet. That night Diao called the Regimental Political Department, and he was told that an investigating group would be sent over soon. At the same time he received an order that required either Diao or me to check in, within a week, at the Divisional Headquarters in Longmen City for a two-month program of studying Engels's *Anti-Dühring*. We were told that the study was designed for officers with a rank above battalion leader.

We talked, and neither of us wanted to leave the battalion at this moment. Diao tried hard to persuade me. "Old Gao, it's a good bargain. The board expenses are one and a half *yuan* a day; there will be six dishes at lunch. Longmen is a big city, where you can go to sports games, movies, and operas. In addition" — he smiled and blinked his eyes — "girls there are pretty, with long braids."

"Old Diao, I appreciate your letting me have such an opportunity, but it's no fun to study there. I can't understand a book like that, no matter how hard I rack my brains. It will be torture. I don't want to make a fool of myself at the Divisional Headquarters. Besides, so many things have to be done here at home. The garages are not roofed yet, and the winter drill will start soon. No, I won't leave at this historic juncture. Old Diao, it's your duty to sharpen your mind. You're the brain of our entire battalion. You're the very person who should go."

We could not persuade each other. Strange to say, next morning a call came from the Regimental Headquarters which ordered me to leave for the study. All right, I didn't complain, because to obey orders is the first principle for an army man. Niu Hsi helped me pack up, and that Saturday I set off for Longmen. Before leaving, I talked to Commissar Diao about Dragon Head's case. "This time," I said, "we must not let him go. We must teach him a lesson so that he will think ten times before doing this sort of thing again. I don't mind if they put him in jail for three months. It seems he should postpone his wedding for a short while. The Dragon's whiskers have to be plucked."

"Old Gao, trust me. I'll handle everything well. Now it's not a matter of hair and skin but a matter of eyes and teeth."

4

Longmen was a good city indeed, very clean. Except that not many girls wore long braids there, everything appeared as Commissar Diao had described. There was fish and meat at lunch every day, and we could even have beer on Saturday evenings. Staying indoors and being fed well, I gained twenty *jin* in those two months. But Engels's book wore us down. The two professors from Longmen City College lectured well and tried hard to make every point plain to us. Still, we couldn't penetrate the book. Shameful as it was, we had to admit that we were too old to become pupils of Marx and Engels.

As soon as the study was over, I returned to Hutou with two other officers in a jeep. At the Regimental Headquarters, I found the chief of the Officer Section, Liu Mingyi, my fellow townsman, and talked to him about Scribe Niu Hsi, for I had heard in Longmen that our regiment was going to send a junior officer to the Second Military Foreign Language Institute to study Russian for three years. Niu Hsi was a good lad and deserved to go to college. He had cut my hair every month for over two years; I was grateful, though I had never mentioned it. Chief Liu seemed to be convinced that Niu Hsi was a proper choice.

"We'll look into his file and make sure that his family background is clean," Liu said.

"Of course it's clean; otherwise how could he be the scribe of my battalion?"

"Old Gao, I know that. This is merely a procedure." He chuckled. "You'll never change a bit and always have a temper like a firecracker."

I took a carton of Peony cigarettes out of my bag and handed it to him. "Here, it's for you, Old Liu."

"Good stuff." He took it with a smile, smelling the end of the carton. "Want to have a drink tonight?"

"No, I have to go back this afternoon."

He narrowed his small eyes and waved his hairy hand, signaling me to come closer. I moved my chair a little forward and rested my elbows on his desk. A young officer was filing something on top of a metal chest five meters away.

"By the way," he said mysteriously, "how do you get along with Diao Shu?"

"Not bad. He's a smart man who knows how to use words."

"Old Gao, we are country boys and don't have many tricks in our heads. Be cautious about Diao."

"Why? What have you heard?"

"Don't ask me why. I cannot tell you. Have you ever thought of going home? I don't mean for a break."

"You mean to be demobilized?"

He smiled, blinking his eyes, and put his index finger across his lips.

I stood up and said, "Old Liu, thank you for the talk."

"I thank you for the cigarettes." He got to his feet. "You can tell Niu Hsi to prepare himself to go."

Coming out of the headquarters at about two o'clock, I strolled to the bus station. I was surprised by what Liu had told me. It seemed that Diao had got up some little maneuvers against me. What did he do? And why did he do it? I could not tell. According to Chief Liu, I might be demobilized. I had never done anything irresponsible or offensive to Diao. How come he held a grudge against me?

The streets were covered with gray snow trampled hard by footsteps and vehicles. Some Korean women went by pulling handcarts, and each cart was loaded with a huge rectangular block of ice. They sang work songs and cracked jokes, which I could tell by their hearty laughter. Trucks blew horns some blocks away; the iron wheels of bullock carts clanked here and there.

At the corner of the movie house, the only one in Hutou Town, about fifty people gathered looking at something. Since the bus would not depart until three, I went over to see what was there. On the bulletin board was a large notice, and some people at the back were pushing forward in order to read its contents. From a distance of twenty meters, I felt that the first picture on the white sheet looked like Dragon Head, so I elbowed my way through the crowd to have a closer view.

It was Dragon Head! His face, crossed by two red strokes, was swollen, and there were some dark patches and small cuts on his forehead and cheeks. His eyes resembled those of a dead fish, while his lips were much thicker than they had been. His long, disheveled hair stuck out in all directions, which made his head seem twice its normal size. Somehow the photograph, once looked at closely, appeared less like Dragon Head than what I had seen from farther back. Beneath him stood a line of characters in boldface: "A Criminal Who Stole Military Equipment." I was shocked and read the charge:

Long Yun, male, 29, from a poor peasant family, has stolen numerous pieces of military equipment, including army clothes, two transceivers, two semiautomatic rifles, etc. The stolen objects have been recovered, and Criminal Long could not deny his crime in the face of the ironclad evidence. For three years, Criminal Long, also called Dragon Head, has commanded his men as a group of idlers, disrupting the agricultural production and sabotaging the national defense. He lorded over several villages and is known in Hutou County as a local tyrant. In order to quiet the anger of the common citizens and to secure the iron bastion of our country's border front, this court has decided to sentence Criminal Long to death. The execution is to be carried out promptly.

With Dragon Head there were three other men to be executed. One had raped two women, another had embezzled twenty thousand *yuan*, and the third had stolen fourteen bicycles.

I started cursing Diao in my mind. Whatever the reason, Dragon Head did not deserve capital punishment. He used to be our friend and would fight any battle for us; now, two years later he was dispatched as an enemy. Even a dog shouldn't be treated this way. During my stay in Longmen I had called Diao a few times and asked about Dragon Head's case at least twice, but each time Diao had assured me that he would handle it properly and advised me to concentrate on the study. Now Dragon Head had been executed; how could Diao call this outcome proper!

When I got back to my battalion, I went to the commissar's office directly. Diao sat at his desk writing something. At the sight of me, he stood up, holding out his hand. "Old Gao, you're back. How was the study?"

"Not bad." We shook hands. "Commissar Diao, I saw the police notice in Hutou Town; so Dragon Head is dead. Why did you do this? It's too despicable!"

"Old Gao, how the hell can you blame me for it?" he said in a high voice. "I didn't want him dead either. I told all the villagers the same thing last week, and now I must repeat it to you: If I could have saved him I would have done it. It was a matter of human life; I want nobody to be killed. He had bad luck and was caught in the middle of the campaign cracking down on crimes. One man who stole bicycles was executed too. But Dragon Head stole guns! If you were here, you couldn't have done anything either."

I went out and flung the door shut. Diao always talked well, but I could not believe him anymore. With his tongue he could take in the villagers from Guanmen but not me this time, although I didn't know how to argue with him.

Having considered what he had said for a short while, I had to admit his words were not totally groundless. Even if he had tried, Diao could by no means have stopped the whole plot. At most, he had served as a secret camera and an official informant on Dragon Head.

Before dinner I got hold of Scribe Niu Hsi and asked him what he knew. We walked out of the barracks. Hard snow squeaked beneath our feet while we were climbing the hill. "The day after you left," Niu Hsi said, "the investigating group arrived, three officers and two policemen. They arrested Ma Ding first. Without much trouble, Ma admitted he had stolen the guns."

"Then how come Ma Ding was not sentenced?"

"They did not allow him to go home that night. The next morning, Dragon Head came, riding the black horse and wearing the two rifles across his back. He asked the investigating group to release Ma Ding and claimed he was responsible for everything. He said he had ordered Ma to steal the guns. They let Ma Ding go and took Dragon Head into custody. Dragon Head confessed that he had been behind everything, including the six hats and the two transceivers. I wrote down what he said during the interrogation, which was very short. He didn't bother to hide anything."

"Do you still have the notes?"

"No. They took them away the next day, together with the two guns. Dragon Head went with them too."

"How did the villagers respond when they heard of his death?"

"They came over, crying and cursing. Wang Si and those militiamen pounded their chests and heads, shouting, 'Brother Dragon's wronged!' The girl, Dragon Head's fiancée, fainted and was carried to our clinic. Commissar Diao spoke with tears in his eyes and calmed them down. He told them that he had a heavy heart over the misfortune too, because he had lost a good friend. But our battalion wasn't involved in the charge and the execution. We had no idea how this had happened. What he said seemed true, so after two hours they went back home."

Gray mist was spreading above the two hundred thatched roofs of Guanmen Village below us. Kerosene lights and candles flickered timidly through the dim curtain of the evening air. A dog was barking. The voices of the children racing about in the streets sounded like birds' chirping in deep woods. I did not want to talk more about Dragon Head. Niu Hsi might as well remain ignorant of the iniquitous reality. So I changed the topic and told him that I had arranged for him to go to college to study Russian. He looked hesitant.

"I know what's in your mind, Little Niu," I said. "You're unsure of yourself."

"No, Commander Gao. I think I can be a good student, as long as I work hard. To be honest, I'm thinking if I should go to college, since I'm already an officer."

"Look at it this way." I smiled. "In a person's life, what part is longer — war or peace?"

"Of course peace is longer."

"Then you need a skill and some knowledge to live in peace. When you're old, do you think you can make a living by carrying a gun like I'm doing now?"

"No, I don't think so."

"Then you should go, must go."

He nodded his head. We turned around and were about to go down the hill. Niu stopped and said, "Commander Gao, I want to tell you something that I don't know if I should."

"What? Tell me."

"Commissar Diao said he had you sent to Longmen."

"What did he tell you exactly?"

"He didn't tell me anything. After the villagers left, I overheard him on the phone: 'Fortunately, we sent Gao Ping away beforehand.'"

"Oh, I understand it now." I was surprised, as the series of events started linking together. We began going down the hill. Now the whole thing became clear in my mind. By ordering me to go to Longmen, the Regimental Political Department had intended to prevent me from interfering with Dragon Head's case; at last, I figured out why among the officers in the study program I was the only battalion leader; the others all had a higher rank. I had not been trusted. Why? Why did Diao treat me as his rival?

Suddenly it dawned on me that Diao Shu was determined to get rid of me, because I happened to know the true history of his family. Anyone with that knowledge could turn him in at any time, so I accidentally became a time bomb in his political and military career. For his own survival, he had to remove me, and the first step to achieve this purpose was to make me appear untrustworthy to our superiors so that nobody would believe what I said. He must have been working on this scheme for quite a while. Undoubtedly, the regimental leaders had already taken me for a troublemaker.

As Chief Liu had revealed to me, three months later I was demobilized.

5

Seven years have elapsed since I left the army. Life has been awfully kind to me. For all these years, I have worked as the chief of the Military Department in our commune. One of my children has gone to college in Tianjin, and the other is doing well in the middle school. In the evenings, I can have a few cups of liquor and chat away with friends till midnight. What else should I ask from life?

Diao Shu is the director of the Political Department of the Third Division now. He is an able man and probably deserves his series of promotions. Niu Hsi, who is still a lad in my eyes, returned to Hutou after graduation and has served as an interpreter in our Fifth Regiment for three years. Last month I received a letter from him. The letter reads as follows:

My Most Respected Commander Gao:
   Please forgive me for my delay in writing to you. How are you now? How are your wife and children?
   Recently I have been terribly busy, for the border is open now. Sometimes I work twelve hours a day. There are so many trade delegations, tourists, and business people that Russian interpreters are in great demand. Many of the local companies and factories turn to me for help when they have business to do with the Russians. Hutou is a peaceful town now — a city, I should say. You can see Russian travelers and shoppers in the streets every day, since there is a daily bus service across the border. Though I'm busy, I won't complain. I have made a lot of money and got nine pairs of leather shoes and two dozen Western suits for free. In fact, I'm thinking of leaving the army now. There's no need to worry about a job. Last month, Harbin Normal Col-

lege contacted me and asked me if I would like to teach Russian in their school.

Dear Commander Gao, how grateful I am to you! Seven years ago, when you wanted me to go to college, I hesitated. It was you who made the decision for me. My family and I will never forget you — our great benefactor.

Here's a small incident, which I think you may be interested in: Last month I accompanied a delegation of our division to Russia to celebrate their Army Day. Vice Divisional Commissar Huang Hsing led the group (you may not know him; he is from the Second Regiment). After the banquet, we had coffee and tea and chatted. Commissar Huang took an envelope from his briefcase and handed it to the Russian officers. Guess what was inside the envelope? A bunch of photographs of Dragon Head! While the Russians were looking at the pictures, Huang explained, "He is the bandit who sank one of your gunboats seven years ago. It was a little unpleasant episode indeed, but we had him executed long ago." I interpreted his words, and the Russians were delighted. Among the photographs there was one showing Dragon Head's blasted face — his forehead was gone. In fact, only I knew that the bandit had been a militia company commander called Dragon Head, but I didn't say anything.

Commander Gao, let my pen stop here for the moment. I will write to you again when I have time.

Please give my regards to your family. May you have good health.

> My Salute,
> A Soldier of Yours
> Niu Hsi
> March 29, Hutou

Niu's letter has made me think a lot about Dragon Head recently. He was a grand fighter, a dragon in Hutou County. He should have fallen on a battlefield.

A Contract

Since the new soldiers came to my squad in February, Gu Gong had never stopped bullying them. Though it was an unstated rule that an older soldier could demand small services from a new soldier, Gu went too far — he would have the two boys wash his bowls and clothes, take his mail to the post office, and even fetch water for him in the morning, as if they had been his orderlies. The new soldiers complained to me twice, and I promised them that I would talk Gu out of his lording over the new comrades, but I didn't have a chance to speak to him before I found myself resorting to force.

It happened one night in early April. After studying the documents issued by the Central Committee on the Ninth Chinese Communist Party Congress, we were preparing to go to bed. Some men went to the washroom down the hall to bathe their feet, while others were taking off their clothes and spreading their quilts.

"Feng Dong," Gu said from the top of the bunk bed, "you forgot to dump the water in my basin."

Sitting beneath Gu, Feng didn't reply and kept unlacing his boots. I hung my hat on a hook on the wall and turned to Gu, who lay on his bed smoking.

"Feng Dong, you bastard of a new soldier." Gu's body jerked up. "Why don't you dump the water?"

"I've never looked after my grandfather that way," Feng said, as if to himself.

"I am your great-grandpa in this squad!"

"Stop it, Gu Gong," I said. "You've gone too far. It's unreasonable to ask others to dump the water you washed your own feet with."

"Oh yeah? I want him to get rid of the water, or somebody will step on it going out to the latrine at night."

"Then it's your duty to dispose of it."

Gu's face turned red. "Who are you, Cheng Zhi? A big squad leader? So what? Do you think you're an officer? How big are you anyway? As big as one of my balls?"

The men around laughed. Enraged, I went up to Gu and pulled him off his bed, together with his quilt and sheet. He fell on the cement floor. Before he could get up, I gave him a kick in the jaw. He jumped to his feet and scuffled toward me, but a few pairs of hands restrained him.

"You beat me," he yelled. "You, a squad leader, beat your soldier." He was struggling to get loose. "Let me go! Let me settle it with him!"

Without a word I walked to the door. I thought it was better for me to stay out of this mess for a moment.

"Cheng Zhi," Gu shouted, "I screw your ancestors one by one! If you are your father's son, don't leave. Let's fight it out."

The sky over Hutou was glimmering with thin mist pierced by stars. The chilly spring wind was rubbing my burning forehead as I went across the drill ground and reached the stream behind our barracks. The thawing ice sent out small noises on the water surface, while some birds were chirping and quacking in the dark. I was grateful to Liu Sheng, the vice squad leader, who had held Gu back before

98

the whole thing could turn ugly. Whatever the reason, as a leader I shouldn't have used force first. Besides, Gu was a stout man and the best fighter in my squad. He came from Shandong Province and had practiced kung fu since childhood. That was why nobody dared confront him. To tell the truth, I was not his match if we fought bare-handed.

I wandered along the stream and through the birch woods until the chilly air began making my skin tingle in my cotton-padded clothes.

When I returned to our room, it was quiet except for several men snoring away. Everybody was fast asleep. I undressed myself and slipped into my bed. Gu stirred, gnashed his teeth, then resumed snoring.

The next day everything went as usual. In the morning we practiced throwing antitank grenades; in the afternoon we worked in our company's vegetable cellar, peeling off rotten cabbage leaves. Gu remained rather placid. I knew the matter was not over, so for an entire day I racked my brain for a solution. Though I did not have a definite idea how to resolve the issue, without doubt it would be better to talk it out than fight it out.

To my surprise, Gu proposed a talk. That evening, when I returned to our room with newspapers and mail, he came to me and said, "Squad Leader Cheng, I need to chat with you."

"All right." I tried to remain calm. "When do you think we should talk?"

"Now." He smiled awkwardly. "Can we go outside?"

"Sure."

All the men watched us in silence as we walked out. Since I had agreed, I had to follow him to any place he thought suitable. The dark evening was a little warm, and the smoky air was motionless. We crossed two rows of poplars and reached the area for gymnastic exercises. He stopped, resting one hand on a parallel bar.

"Cheng Zhi, I never thought you were so fierce." A mysterious grin spread on his egg-shaped face.

"Gu Gong, we joined the army in the same year, and I didn't mean to embarrass you in front of the new soldiers —"

"You beat me! Damn you, even my parents never kicked me like that."

"Listen to me —"

"You were so wild last night. Now, let yourself run wild again."

"What do you want?"

"I want to settle it with you now. Let's go a few rounds." His small eyes were shimmering in the dark while his hands were rubbing each other, as if he were preparing himself for a wrestling contest.

I tried hard to stay coolheaded. "Listen, Gu Gong, we are revolutionary soldiers and don't play games like hooligans. I'm not good at doing things in your style and can only fight in the soldier's way, so I refuse to 'play' with you."

"You chicken. All right then, let your grandpa teach you manners." He was moving toward me.

"Halt!" a few voices shouted. Vice Squad Leader Liu Sheng, Zhao Min, and Wang Longyun emerged. They stopped Gu, pacifying him and hauling him back to the quarters. Though his elbows were struggling, Gu's legs seemed ready to give in as he followed them away.

Meanwhile he kept cursing, "Chicken, chicken. You dare not fight. All you dare do is steal a blow when others are unprepared. Chicken, how come you lead us men?"

They were out of the drill ground now. I stood there alone, feeling my blood boil. What should I do? Fight bare-handed with him? If I could not beat him, what was the use of fighting that way? They had all seen us just now and must have believed I was afraid of him. What should I do? I had to find a way to stop him. How?

Ten minutes later I rejoined my squad. When I entered the room, the men suddenly stopped talking. Feng Dong was gaping at Gu Gong, who smirked silently while exhaling smoke. I picked up a poker, drilled a few holes through the cinders in the stove, and added three shovels of coal to the flames, which began crackling. Raising my head, I saw Gu standing erect against the pillar of his bed, his chin up and his eyes peering at me. Nobody had made a sound since I came in.

I sat down at the desk, took out a sheet of paper, and started writing. I wrote as follows:

This evening, Soldier Gu Gong challenged Cheng Zhi, Leader of the Eighth Squad of the First Company, to fight bare-handed with him. All having been considered, we realized that a melee does not suit the style of revolutionary soldiers, so we have decided to do it with weapons. Also having considered bullets must be saved for the Russians, we have chosen to use bayonets. When we begin, the whole squad will be present, and we will not stop until one of us cannot resist anymore. If either of us gets wounded or killed in this practice, the victim himself is solely responsible for such a mishap. This contract, drawn on April 15, is here signed by both

Cheng Zhi   Gu Gong

I signed my name but couldn't find red ink paste for a fingerprint, so I used a black ink stick instead and put my thumbprint beneath my name. Then I handed the sheet to Liu Sheng. "Read it out to the whole squad."

While Liu was reading in a metallic voice, I went to the gun rack and picked up a semiautomatic rifle. The bayonet was pressed down between my forefinger and thumb. Its blade drew a semicircle in the air, and with a clatter it settled firmly on the muzzle. Wiping the bluish bayonet with a rag, I looked at Gu Gong, whose face had turned sallow. Tiny beads of sweat were breaking out on his forehead, and his eyes fixed on the floor. My heart was fluttering.

"I'll wait for you fellows on the drill ground." I opened the door and went out.

Once in the hall, I heard Gu cry out inside the room, "He's an orphan, but I have my old parents at home!" What he said was true.

The gun seemed weightless on my back as I paced about under the poplars, rolling cigarettes and smoking. The breeze was fanning my face and hair. It was good to feel and smell the approach of the spring, which day and night was creeping from the south to the north — to us, and then to Siberia. The purple sky, so vast, curved in every direction toward the serrated hilltops in both China and Russia. I waited at the drill ground for half an hour, until Vice Squad Leader Liu appeared from the dark.

"Gu Gong has buried his head in his quilt," he said with a smile.

"I'd better not go in now. You stay with the squad. If you want me, go to the study room for me. All right?"

"Sure."

I thought that our company leaders would reprimand me and order me to write out self-criticism for impairing our solidarity, but when I reported the incident the next day, they didn't look worried at all. Secretary Ling Ping screwed up one of his eyes and said, "Comrade Cheng Zhi, remember: Never strike the first blow."

Two months later, I was promoted to command the Second Platoon.

Miss Jee

After we cleaned the classroom and spread rice straw along the wall to make a large bed, we — the Thirteenth Squad — had our first meeting. Sitting on the squared timber nailed to the floor to contain the straw, we were introducing ourselves. The squad leader said his name was Lu Hai. Unlike us recruits, he had served in the Fifth Regiment for two years.

Then we introduced ourselves, each in two or three sentences. Jee was the last to speak. "I'm Jee Jun, nineteen, an orphan, from Yushu County, Jilin Province. I joined the army because I'm grateful to the Party and the people who brought me up. The Russian Social-Imperialists have massed over a million troops along our border and attempt to invade our country, so it's my duty to come and defend the Motherland with my blood and life!"

None of us had expected this slender lad to speak so well. His thin lips quivered after he stopped, and his long eyes gleamed.

Impressed, some of us struck up a conversation with him after the meeting. I thought Jee must have been a high school graduate, unlike me, who had gone through elementary school only. I wanted to get close to him but didn't know how.

In the evening we studied newspapers together, Guan Chi and Jee Jun by turns reading out a long editorial, "Resolutely Punish the Russian Chauvinists." After the study, we were preparing for bed. Wu Desheng smiled to himself, still sitting on the timber. "Jee Jun, you sounded funny when you read aloud, you know."

"How?" Jee asked, unlacing his boots.

"You sounded like a girl."

"Damn your mother!"

We all laughed. Wu's eyelids were flapping. "It has nothing to do with my mother. You really sound like a girl. Don't you think so, Fan Hsiong?"

He asked me, but before I could answer, Wang Fukai cut in, "Look, he looks like a girl too."

"I look like your grandpa!"

We laughed again. Jee indeed resembled a girl, with a pale face, curved eyebrows, pink cheeks, slim hands and feet. "What a discovery," Song Ang said. "We have a young lady among us."

"Miss Jee, nice to meet you." Guan Chi stretched out his hand.

"Miss Jee, how do you do?"

"Welcome to our squad, Miss Jee."

"Can I help you, miss?"

"I screw all your mothers!"

Squad Leader Lu intervened. "Enough, men." He turned to Jee. "Don't take it to heart, Jee Jun. They were just joking, no hard feelings."

We didn't sleep well the first night. At eleven sharp, a horn burst out honking in the corridor like a crazy goose, and we all jumped up groping for our clothes in the dark. The electricity was out. Squad Leader Lu said in a subdued voice, "Emergency muster! Pack up your stuff, take your weapons, and follow me out."

We were fumbling in the large straw bed. Zhang Min cursed and couldn't find his socks; his large body knocked me about. Jee moaned weirdly while struggling to put on his clothes. A mug dropped on the floor. "You took my hat, Song Ang." That was Wu Desheng's thick voice.

"Quiet!" the squad leader said.

I forgot how to tie up a field pack. Trying twice without success, I gave up, simply binding my quilt and pillow into a roll. Thank Heaven, I found my mittens in the straw. With the baggage on my back, I rushed to the rack for my rifle.

Following Squad Leader Lu, we ran into the starry night. The ground was slippery and the air piercingly cold. "Put on your nose cover," he ordered. That was a narrow piece of fur buttoned to the earflaps of a hat to prevent the nose from freezing. We executed the orders while running. Many squads were already gathered on the playground. The second we reached there, Squad Leader Lu ran to Company Commander Su to report our arrival. Meanwhile, two more squads were coming, their boots drumming the icy ground.

"Comrades," Commander Su called out, "we just received orders. A fight has broken out at the border. The Regimental Headquarters ordered us to reach the front within an hour." He paused, then shouted, "Right face!"

We turned. He ran to the head of our lines. "Squad One, follow me!"

A moment later we were running in a single line along a path toward Hutou Town, which was five *li* away from the middle school where we were quartered. The night was glimmering slightly, and a few waves of snow dust were shoving one another in the lazy wind. In the northern sky the Big Dipper, silvery and blinking, stretched to the distant hills. It was quiet everywhere except for our boots treading the snow and the words passed in muffled voices, "Close up!" or "Watchword: Victory."

To our surprise, we did not continue to run north toward the border after we entered Hutou Town. Instead we circled around a few blocks, then dashed back to the school. My eyes were fixed on Jee Jun's field pack in front of me, as though his baggage were able to pull me forward, while my legs went weak and no longer felt like my own.

When we returned, all the lights were on in the school-house. Our room was a mess. On the floor were scattered mugs, canteens, pillows, toothbrushes, socks, photographs, ammunition belts, notebooks, mittens, shirts.

"What's this, Fan Hsiong?" Zheng Yuan asked me and slapped my back. "Is this a field pack or a hay bundle?"

Seeing my baggage roll, some of my comrades whooped and a few applauded. I was annoyed but said nothing.

"Look!" Song Ang cried, "look at Jee's butt."

We all turned and found the fly of Jee's trousers gaping on his behind. The entire squad broke out laughing. Jee swung around and dropped his hips on the radiator beneath the window. "I, I had no time to, to put it right." He flushed.

"You don't need the fly anyway," Song Ang said, blowing his broad nose with a handkerchief. We laughed some more.

Soon afterwards, a couplet began circulating in the Recruit Company. It went:

> Miss Jee toured the borderline
> With the fly open on her behind.

The doggerel at once established Jee's nickname among the soldiers. He had no choice but to accept it. Calling him Miss Jee, we bore no malice against him; the recruits' life was hard, and we needed some fun.

In the beginning, whenever we talked about weapons and wars, Jee would join us, but he was ignorant of military science. Though he said he wanted to fight the Russians, he was not cut out to be a soldier at all; he couldn't even tell a tactic from a strategy — he used the two words as if they were identical in meaning. Unable to contribute anything to our discussion of battles and weaponry, he soon withdrew to a corner to read alone or write in his green notebook. He kept a diary.

Despite his fondness for books, Jee was not learned. In fact, he had gone to middle school for only one year. Quite a few of us were better scholars than he was. For example, Song Ang, a sprinter who could do the hundred-meter dash in 11.9 seconds, was the most knowledgeable about weaponry and wars. Because his father was a commander on a missile destroyer at Port Arthur, Ang had read a lot of the navy's classified books and documents. He provided us with information on different types of artillery and warships, especially the Russians' nuclear submarines carrying intercontinental missiles. Guan Chi also knew a lot. He looked scholarly and would put on steel-rimmed glasses when reading. In addition, he was an experienced fighter. He told us that at home he and his pals had once driven a T-34 tank on the streets and fired its two machine guns at the buildings occupied by those revolutionary rebels who held a different theory of revolution from theirs. They had also raided restaurants at midnight and carried back fried dough sticks and roasted chickens on their bayonets.

I slept between Jee Jun and Zhang Min, who had been my classmate back home. Zhang snored a lot at night. It didn't bother me, since I was told that I also made noises. Jee didn't snore, but he was often restless in his sleep. He'd hit my chest with his elbow, or kick my thigh, or give me a jab in the back. When I complained about this "night fight," my comrades would say I was lucky to sleep and frolic with a young lady every night. Then they'd ask Jee, "Would you like to go with me, Miss Jee?" "Can I share the bed with you tonight, Miss Jee?" "Miss, how do you like me as a young man?" "How much do you charge per night, miss?" Jee never answered and merely glared at the questioners.

One night, he roused me. He pulled my arm and whispered, "Look, look at that girl over there. Isn't she beautiful? Like a little willow." He smiled, then murmured something inaudible.

I shook off his hand and cursed, "Damn you, taking home a bride in a dream."

He turned over and went back to sleep.

The next day I told the squad about Jee's midnight fantasy. They sat around and asked him what the girl had looked like and why he'd compared her to a willow. What kind of willow exactly? A weeping willow? A silky willow? A red willow? Jee was mad at me because he couldn't remember the dream and believed I had made it up. "Fan Hsiong, I screw your sisters! You, such a small boy, can tell a lie as big as Heaven!"

I didn't argue and merely said, "I don't have a sister."

"Even if he had," Wu put in, "how can you do that, miss?"

"I did it to your mother!"

"Let's see how big you are."

We laughed heartily. Wu spilt the tobacco he had been rolling into a cigarette with his large hands.

Like us, Jee was very interested in women. He claimed he had a fiancée, whose father was the commune chairman at home. Nobody believed him, though. I once flipped through his diary secretly, to see if he really had a girlfriend. To my dismay, almost everything he had written was related to fighting the Russian Revisionists and guarding the northern frontier. In one item he even said, "I won't regret it if I die ten times for our great Motherland." I never mentioned the contents of his diary to anybody, though impressed by his sincerity.

Jee often argued with Zheng Yuan about women, bragging

that in his hometown there were lots of young beauties whose faces were as white and soft as fresh tofu. It was this habit that made him an enemy of Zheng Yuan. According to Zheng's own words, which must be taken with caution, Zheng's maternal grandfather was a top general in North Korea, so his mother was Korean whereas his father was Chinese. In other words, he was a hybrid. He tried convincing us that his mother was the most beautiful woman on earth. I doubted it, because he was so short; though eighteen, two years older than myself, he was three inches shorter. How could a beautiful woman, a general's daughter, give birth to such a thick-boned, bean-eyed, toothy dwarf? Jee never believed a word of what Zheng said and always challenged him. "Don't boast about your mother. Just show us her picture. Let's see what a goddess she is."

Of course Zheng was never able to produce such a photo. He would fight Jee on the drill ground, since Jee was the worst soldier in our company. When they were paired off for bayonet practice, Zheng would stab Jee's forearms and hands with the rubber head of his wooden gun. He could do it easily, and Jee simply couldn't parry a jab. Once hit, he would throw his weapon to the ground and squat down, rubbing the wound and calling Zheng Barbarian Bastard. Within a week some black patches appeared on his arms and the backs of his hands. Later he just refused to practice with Zheng, and our squad leader had to keep them separate.

It was even worse that Jee could not throw a grenade. However hard he tried, at most he threw it sixteen meters. Seeing it land so close, Zheng Yuan, the "Little Cannon" who could throw it forty-five meters easily would say, "I can send it that far with either of my feet."

The minimum requirement was thirty meters. I made only twenty-eight; though both Jee and I couldn't pass, nobody laughed at me — I was close. Besides, I was three years younger than Jee. When it came to the final test with the real grenade, everybody was afraid to be grouped with Jee. Because we two had the weakest arms, Platoon Leader Ding made Jee and me the last pair to throw.

The range was in a cornfield beyond the southern hill. There was a deep ditch at the end of the furrows, so we could hide ourselves in it when the grenade throwers carried out the test in the field. Two by two my comrades took their turns. Everybody passed and said the real grenade was lighter than the fakes used for training. When our turn came, I had got somewhat used to the explosions, and my heart stopped kicking. Still, I felt uneasy about Jee. Platoon Leader Ding handed Jee and me each a grenade and pointed to the large triangle he had drawn with his boots in the snow-covered field. "Stay calm and throw it into the target."

Jee was on my right, the platoon leader on my left. We twisted off the caps and hooked the rings onto our little fingers.

"Ready —" Platoon Leader Ding raised his hand. "Throw!"

The grenades flew off our hands, swishing like flapping wings. We both lay prone immediately. The platoon leader fell on my back, covering me. One grenade exploded in the distance, then the other thundered right in front of us. My eyes blurred, I was deafened. Smoke and snow dust filled the air; my hat was gone, and I felt my neck tight and numb.

"Killed!" A vague voice came from the ditch a few seconds later. "Hey, are you all right?"

No answer. Platoon Leader Ding managed to sit up. "Terrible! My grandma, terrible."

Some men ran over. Jee and I were still lying on the ground. He was motionless. "What happened?" our squad leader asked. I turned over and tried to get up.

"Terrible, he threw it only nine meters." The platoon leader pointed at Jee.

"Are you all right?" Song Ang asked me. He took off the slips of corn stubble from my hat, which he had recovered from God knows where, and put it on my head.

"I don't know," I moaned. "I feel queasy."

Meanwhile Jee was helped up. He sat on the ground, his face covered with blood. "Hey, bring over a first-aid dressing," Guan shouted to the men in the ditch.

"Jee doesn't look injured," Song Ang said.

"No," Jee said. "I'm all right, not injured. My nose has a bleeding problem. Sorry, I didn't throw it well. Rub some snow on my forehead." He sounded so calm, like an experienced soldier.

At once everybody relaxed, but we remained silent as if we had yet to recover from the shock. I was told that my grenade had reached twenty-nine meters, within the target; since it was only one meter short of the requirement, Platoon Leader Ding let me pass. I was happy, though a fragment of Jee's grenade had pierced a hole in my fur hat. Jee alone flunked the test.

Before long another two lines were composed about him. In addition to the former couplet, the company now chanted this one:

> Miss Jee threw a hand grenade
> Only to have her looks remade.

As his fame increased, Jee grew reticent. Even if somebody hummed the couplets in his face, he wouldn't respond. At night he became less fitful than before and seldom woke me. Still many of us kept teasing him; some even brought him soft toilet paper for his periods, or asked him to sew on a button, or claimed to be his bridegrooms.

One thing we could not complain about Jee was that he

did not eat much. Except for him, all the new soldiers ate like wolves. At every meal we bolted down the first bowl of sorghum and refilled it as many times as possible. The Recruit Company was a temporary unit without any surplus provisions, and most of the new soldiers were from the countryside and had no grease in the stomachs, so we ate and ate and ate. Lacking fresh vegetables, a month later over a dozen soldiers suffered from snow blindness, and many had chapped scrotums and walked bowlegged. Our regiment made an urgent request to the Divisional Headquarters for vitamins.

But there was no problem with Jee; it was as though he belonged to a different species. He always ate two bowls at a meal, while the rest of us devoured at least twice as much and still felt hungry at drill. I never heard Jee complain of hunger. Neither could I tell whether he ate like that because of his small appetite or because of his healthy diet. In any case, he didn't eat like a man.

One Tuesday morning, we had a meeting which was designed to recall the past miseries and appreciate the present happiness. At lunch only bitter buns, made of husks and wild herbs, were served as a sample of what life had tasted like in the Old China. We couldn't eat them. Most of us threw them away secretly, but Jee chewed and swallowed his three buns with relish. In our squad only he finished the meal. That afternoon at drill, when we complained that our stomachs were rumbling, he smiled and said that we had been spoiled by our parents and that we had no idea what genuine suffering was like. Little wonder we were such rascals.

But his euphoria lasted only a few hours. The dinner was a sample of the present sweetness, so there was plenty of good food — fried pork, bean sprouts with scrambled eggs, noodles, and stewed pollack. Because we hadn't eaten lunch, the spacious dining room instantly turned into a battlefield. The major fight was waged around two huge field caldrons containing noodles. Waves of men, bowls and chopsticks in hands, charged, plundered as much as possible, then withdrew with filled bowls to the dining tables. I pushed forward, waving my chopsticks in the air fearful of poking somebody's eyes. When I had almost reached a caldron, Jee emerged from the left flank, panting hard and moving ahead. I bent forward to load my bowl; so did Jee. All of a sudden, noodles splashed on the floor and people dispersed. I stepped back, wiping my face with the back of my hand, and found Jee sitting in the caldron, bareheaded and pop-eyed. God knew how he had got in there.

He scrambled out, his trousers mottled with noodles and cabbage leaves. Without a word he dashed out of the dining room. Squad Leader Lu, putting down his bowl and spoon, followed him immediately. Jee's fur hat was still floating in the caldron like a drowned chicken. Laughter and cries rang out. Many men went up to the mess to have a better look.

Then Political Instructor Ni arrived and reprimanded us: "Are you revolutionary soldiers or not? Where's your discipline? You pushed your dear comrade-in-arms into the hot noodles. Where is your proletarian affection? Don't you feel ashamed? Won't you suffer from a stomachache, having such noodles inside you?"

Most of us could not eat for a while, because if we had opened our mouths we would have broken into laughter. Song Ang and I put down our bowls and went back to see Jee. Squad Leader Lu was sitting with him in our room, which smelled of soy sauce. Jee, in his underpants, was weeping, his boots and cotton-padded trousers on the radiator; seeing us, he turned his face to the window. Song Ang said, "Don't take it so hard, Jee Jun. Instructor Ni scolded those men in the dining room."

"It wasn't your fault," I said.

Jee didn't respond. Unable to do anything, we returned to the dining room to finish dinner and to bring some food back for Jee and our squad leader. In there people talked and smiled while eating. "Miss Jee" was discussed at every table.

Shortly afterwards, another couplet was composed. The little doggerel got two more lines:

> Miss Jee, loving noodle soup,
> Dived into a caldron in a swoop.

Now he was famous. Soldiers from other platoons would come under any pretext to have a look at him. Most often they would say they came to visit their fellow townsmen. Our squad became the most popular spot in the company. In addition to Jee, Guan was a wonderful storyteller and would entertain the visitors with ancient chivalric legends.

The most difficult course in our training was Russian — I mean for those of us who didn't know the language. The textbook was not big — only eight pages long and three by four inches. It consisted of fifteen sentences altogether, such as "Hands up!" "Don't move!" "This is China's territory!" "Don't waste your life for the Russian Revisionist Imperialists!" "Down with the New Czar!" "Put down your arms and we'll spare your lives!" "Follow me!"

Guan and Song had studied Russian in middle school, so those sentences were nothing for them, but the rest of us had to labor day and night to remember every sound in each word. We marked every Russian syllable with a Chinese character and then tried to memorize the characters in a meaningless order. When we shouted out the Russian words on the drill ground, nobody could understand them, let alone obey the orders correctly. Wu once burst into tears, because that afternoon somehow his tongue simply couldn't work out a Russian sentence and even his Chinese was broken and incomprehensible. In Jee's words, "it was like having a donkey's penis in his mouth." He kept gnashing his gums at us for hours.

Besides our two Russian experts, Guan and Song, Jee did really well. He was probably the best among us, the ignorant ones. Of course he worked on it harder than we did. He could rap out every syllable clearly, though his sentences tended to remain broken. Wu often grabbed him to practice Russian together. Jee's voice was thin and suave, while Wu's was thick and hoarse. Whenever the two practiced in the corridor, we would prick up our ears, listening. "No, not like that," Jee would say. "Don't mumble. You must shout and let your voice scare them."

Apparently Jee was pleased with his Russian, though he dared not demonstrate his achievement in the presence of Song and Guan. Song once offered to teach him a few more sentences, but Jee neither accepted nor refused. He merely said, "Let me think about it."

"Don't you want to know some truly interesting words?" Guan broke in, winking at Jee.

"I want to know everything about your mother."

We laughed.

"Miss Jee," Guan went on, "if you really want to know those words, you must stop being so promiscuous and marry me first. Otherwise how can I make you understand those secret words? Oh, I'm sorry. I forgot you're not a virgin anymore. Of course you can understand."

The whole room rang with laughter. Jee remained silent, glaring at Guan with his teeth gritted.

In the final week of the training, we undertook a forced march. This time everything was described to us in advance — the route, the task, and the time were all clear. After dinner, everybody was given two steamed buns for the night. Like most of my comrades, I ate them promptly, believing it better to carry them inside than on my back. Jee didn't eat his. He was always more calculating than we were.

At eight-thirty we set out south. The snow was deep; the air smelled of birch and pine. Fully equipped, we walked and ran in turn through fields, valleys, hills, woods. Our task was to reach a hill in the Six-Finger Mountain by eleven and surround and wipe out the Russian paratroops.

The wind slacked off while the temperature was dropping. A silver moon swayed in the cloudless sky. Time and again, flocks of crows and pheasants were roused by us, darting away into the dark. A pack of wolves was howling in a distant valley.

It was ten-fifteen and we still had nine *li* ahead. Our pace was picking up; we moved at the double, which gradually turned to a sprint. "Close up!" Platoon Leader Ding ordered under his breath. We were running desperately. The air was vibrating with the commotion caused by our boots. Somebody's canteen dropped on the ground and was kicked off, clattering down a cliff. Soon the mountain emerged like a gigantic mushroom in the sky in front of us.

At eleven sharp the bugle blared out and we charged up the hill. Somebody shouted in Russian, "Put down your arms!" Then many kinds of Russian words were echoing in the mountain.

Soon I felt top-heavy, as though the earth was shifting under my feet. Jee was ahead of me, his rifle across his field pack and his hands grabbing branches to pull himself upward. He climbed very slowly.

We were less than a hundred meters from the summit now. Suddenly three red flares pierced the sky, their blazing tails drawing large question marks in the dark space. Below them everything turned pink and distinct for a few seconds.

This meant that the enemy was eliminated and that our men had reached the top. I climbed with all my strength and caught up with Jee. He was staggering; he stopped, holding the branches of a juniper with both hands.

"Jee, hurry up," I said.

He shook his head; his body seemed to reel. Zheng Yuan came up and slapped Jee on the back. "Need help?"

Jee shook his head again. Zheng went on climbing. I was desperate and cried at Jee, "Come on, let's go!"

Jee pressed his fist against his stomach. "Oh, I'm so hungry!"

"Take a bite of your bun, quick." I fished a bun out of his bag, but I didn't raise it to his mouth. It was frozen as hard as stone. "You can't eat this. Come, let's go."

He looked tearful, but he struggled to move up. The second he let go of the branches, he fell into a swoon, rolling down the slope together with a few rocks. I was scared and shouted, "Squad Leader Lu, Jee Jun fainted! Come over here and help!"

A few men climbed down looking for Jee. Across the hill, one voice after another cried, "Miss Jee fainted!" There were happy whoops and laughter everywhere. At once, everybody seemed to forget his fatigue.

Fortunately, Jee was not hurt. When we were carrying him down the hill, I was surprised that his cotton-padded jacket and trousers were all wet; even his fur hat was soaked with sweat. He must have been extremely weak. Even if he had eaten those buns before the departure, still he might not have been able to make the march. We wrapped him up in two overcoats and put him on a horse cart, which carried him and the cooks directly home.

The next morning, I was amazed to see Jee get up as usual and do the early morning exercises. He was tough.

His fainting in the mountain gave rise to another couplet.

This time I didn't participate in making it, though. Zheng Yuan was the most active one, but he was no poet and couldn't contribute a word. Song Ang and Guan Chi were the major authors. Now the Miss Jee poem had its fourth stanza:

> Miss Jee, tiny appetite,
> Cried for a bun in a fight.

One afternoon Wang Fukai complained that the doggerel didn't feel finished. Everyone agreed, but nobody could add anything to it, hard as they tried. Poetry must reflect real life; without an actual occurrence, however smart they were, those poetic brains couldn't create another good couplet about Jee. If what the lines described had not actually happened, none of us would accept them, because we could never libel Jee.

In several days we would leave for different units. Quite a few men were busy working on a new couplet, but to no avail. Not until the farewell dinner was there a breakthrough in the project.

Each squad was to eat the last dinner in their own room. We brought back dishes and rice in washbasins and liquor in thermos bottles. At last, we were able to eat and drink our fill. Certainly not everybody was happy during the last days, because some of us were assigned to good units while others had to go to bad ones. Song Ang, Zheng Yuan, and I were going to the Artillery Battalion at Guanmen Village, Guan Chi and Wang Fukai to the Fourth Company at Fangshi Valley, Zhang Min to the Reconnaissance Company at Lujia Village, Jee Jun to the Ninth Company in Mati Mountain. Lucky for Wu Desheng, he would go to the Transportation Platoon at the Regimental Headquarters. This meant he was going to learn how to drive a truck. Such a bulky fellow, he should have driven a tank, as we had thought. Wang Fukai was scared, because his company was stationed at the front. On our way to the kitchen to bring back cabbage salad, he said to me, "I must write home and ask my dad to have me transferred back inland." His father was a divisional chief of staff in the Thirty-ninth Army. Actually, Jee's company was at the most forward position, only four *li* from the border, but he did not look disturbed. It seemed he would be the first of us to meet the Russians, and he was ready for it.

Since the night march, Jee had seldom said an unnecessary word; whenever free, he read by himself. Unlike us, he had more time because he didn't write letters. In the eight weeks of the training he wrote only once, to his commune. Now, even a few minutes before the farewell dinner, he sat there alone by the window poring over Chairman Mao's poetry. Though he looked uninterested in the feast, I caught him glancing at the liquor and dishes on the floor.

"Put that book away, Miss Jee," Guan said. Then he turned to us. "Now begins the banquet."

We all stood up, including Jee, and raised our mugs. Squad Leader Lu proposed: "May every one of you have a future as broad as ten thousand *li!*"

"Glasses dry!"

"Glasses dry!"

We all drained our mugs. Everybody turned to Jee; to our amazement, his was also empty. "You're good, Miss Jee," Wu said. "Come, let's have another for our friendship."

"Who's your friend?" Jee refilled his mug and looked fierce. "Come on, glasses dry. Everybody, not only Hog Wu."

We all emptied another mug, then began attacking the stewed pork and the fried yellow croakers. I felt sick, having never drunk so much; I sat down and tried to eat some scrambled eggs and mushrooms. Meanwhile, the others gobbled and gulped, laughing and talking about their units and possible job assignments.

We hadn't expected Jee to have a large capacity for alcohol. After four or five mugs, most of us could no longer stand. Only Song Ang and Wu Desheng accompanied Jee drinking now, though nobody ever gave up eating. Jee challenged them again. Rolling his round eyes, Song said, "Wait a minute, I need to pee. Wait until I'm back with more room inside." He turned to me. "Little Fan, do you want to pee?"

I slouched out with him, fearing Jee would dare me to drink more. We did not go to the latrine but just urinated outside the entrance of the schoolhouse, since we were leaving and wouldn't have to do the cleaning ourselves. As our urine was drilling holes in the ice, Song yawned and chanted:

> Hot pee melts a thousand feet of ice;
> Good manure increases tons of rice.

"Wonderful poetry," I said. The cold wind was hissing.

"Too bad we can't finish the Miss Jee poem," he replied.

When we returned, only Jee stood in the room. Wu was prone on the floor. "He's defeated." Jee pointed at Wu. "None of you is a man. Song Ang, it's your turn."

Song grinned and took a thermos bottle. "Let's u-use this bigger mug, Miss Jee."

"All right." Jee picked up a thermos from the floor. They clinked and began drinking. Both of them, each with one arm akimbo, stood there as if blowing thick bugles.

Three minutes later, Song collapsed on the floor; neither of them drained the thermos bottle. Jee looked at me, his face stained with tears and liquor. I thought he would challenge me, but he didn't.

"I screw all your ancestors!" he cursed. "I came to fight

the Russians, but I have to fight you hooligans!" He smashed the thermos on the floor. Our squad leader moaned in response to the bang, but he couldn't sit up.

Jee was wailing. "Ah, if you're your fathers' sons, get up, let's drink like men! Zheng Yuan, you said I have a tiny appetite. Come, let's eat together."

To our surprise, Zheng sat up and said calmly, "Miss Jee, let's eat." He took a bowl of rice, and so did Jee. Then they started eating.

A few of us managed to sit up watching the contest. In no time they finished the rice, but Zheng gave up and said he had a stomachache. Who wouldn't? Everyone had already eaten many bowls.

Then Wu got up from the floor and challenged, "Miss Jee, let's see who can eat more hot pepper."

"All right, I'll accompany you to your end." Jee breathed rather heavily, his nose running.

They each had half a bowl of rice and covered it to the rim with chili powder. They mixed the white and the red together in the bowls and then set about eating. Wu moved his chopsticks slowly, while Jee gobbled with bubbling noises.

All of a sudden Jee dropped to the floor; the bowl bounced to the radiator and shattered. His legs were twisting as he turned from side to side screaming for help. We were scared, and had no idea what to do.

Song Ang got up and moved close. "What's wrong, Jee?"

"Oh, oh I busted my stomach!"

Squad Leader Lu climbed out of bed and went up to him. "Roll over." He helped him turn prone. "There, try to throw up. Throw up as much as you can."

"Oh I can't. My throat is clogged. Oh, oh —" Jee was sweating all over; his lips were purple and his face as pale as wax. Squad Leader Lu staggered out to call for an ambulance.

We were scared out of our drunkenness and gathered around, but all we could do was spread a cold, wet towel on his forehead. Meanwhile, he never stopped groaning and twitching. "Jee, are you all right?" Wu asked.

No answer. We thought he was dying. I remembered a soldier in the other recruit company who had stuffed himself to death with mutton dumplings and apples. His stomach had been as big as a basin when the doctor had taken it out.

The ambulance came and took Jee to the Regimental Infirmary. Our company's medic went with him, while we waited anxiously to hear about his condition. Late that night we were informed that Jee was out of danger. I thought they would cut him open, but they didn't. Instead they made him drink a lot of soybean oil to induce him to vomit, and they also gave him enemas. Though stable now, he had to be kept under observation for a few days.

Before we set out for our new units the next day, we had no chance to say good-bye to Jee. Every one of us donated a *yuan,* a sixth of our monthly allowance. Since they both were to stay at the Regimental Headquarters, Squad Leader Lu Hai and Wu Desheng would buy whatever they thought appropriate with the money and visit Jee Jun on our behalf. They were to tell him that we all would like to keep in touch with him.

The farewell dinner had provided those poetic brains with rich material for another couplet. With ease they completed the doggerel, which now went:

> Miss Jee toured the borderline
> With the fly open on her behind.

> Miss Jee threw a hand grenade
> Only to have her looks remade.

> Miss Jee, loving noodle soup,
> Dived into a caldron in a swoop.

Miss Jee, tiny appetite,
Cried for a bun in a fight.

Miss Jee, drinking like a whale,
Still can't prove she is a male.

Everybody was impressed by the rhyme in the last couplet. We all wrote the poem down in our notebooks, as though it was our common heritage, which we would carry to the battlefield.

A Lecture

Again it was time for studying the Party's history. Secretary Si Ma Lin of the Radio Company had to rewrite his lectures, because the significance and nature of some events in the textbook changed each year. For example, the year before, Lin Biao had been "the Wise Marshal," but the next year he became a traitor throughout the history of the Chinese Communist Party. If only there were a definitive textbook, then Si Ma would be able to prepare his lectures once and for all. That would save him a lot of time.

Recently he was tickled by an idea. It was said that a retired cadre, Liu Baoming, had been a participant in the Long March. Why not invite him to talk to the company? To begin this year's study with a vivid lecture would at least arouse the soldier's interest in the Party's history. In addition, Si Ma felt that there might be something worth writing in the old revolutionary's experience. He would take down what the old man said. If lucky, he might be able to cast the talk into an article and have it published somewhere. That would be a good way of showing the caliber of his pen to his superiors in the Divisional Political Department.

He discussed the matter with Company Commander Pei Ding. Though lukewarm about the idea, Pei agreed to have

Old Liu over. The two company leaders were on uneasy terms because Si Ma was one rank higher than Pei, earning nine *yuan* more a month.

Si Ma went to Liu's house, which was just a few blocks away from the barracks, to invite Liu officially. The old man agreed to come, and Si Ma promised that he would send an automobile to pick him up at one-thirty on Friday afternoon.

On Thursday, Si Ma called the Divisional Headquarters to arrange a jeep for Liu, but he was told that nothing would be available on Friday. Fortunately, the Radio Company had a Yellow River truck that could carry eight tons, so he dispatched it to the Lius' the next day.

After the soldiers took their seats in the meeting room, Si Ma went to the front and said, "Comrades, this is our first lecture on the Party's history. Our company is very fortunate today to have an old Red Army man to talk to us about the Long March. First, let me introduce to you Comrade Liu Baoming." He raised his hand politely, palm to the ceiling, pointing at the guest on a front seat. His chin also jutted at him.

Liu's white head rose before the soldiers. Many of them were surprised to find that the Red Army man was the small man who played chess with those retired workers near the entrance of the Divisional Headquarters every day. Liu gave a smile to the audience, waving his shriveled hand sideways. He sat down.

"As you all know" — Si Ma spoke again — "the Long March is a heroic epic that shocked the whole world. Our Great Leader Chairman Mao led the Red Army to climb the snow mountains, cross the grass marshes, fight the warlords' troops and Chiang Kai-shek's armies, and trek through eleven provinces; all together they walked twenty-five thousand *li*. The Long March saved our army, our Party, our revolution, and our country. When it started from Jiangxi Province in 1934, the Red Army had over three hundred thousand men; but when it reached Northern Shanxi the next year, there were only thirty thousand left. Comrades, so many Revolutionary Martyrs sacrificed their precious young lives for the liberation of the Chinese people. Today, four decades later, only hundreds of the Long March participants are alive in China. Our honored guest today, Comrade Liu Baoming, is one of them.

"Comrades, we must cherish this opportunity to learn about our Party's glorious history. We must listen to him carefully and take down everything he says. Now, let us welcome Comrade Old Liu."

In a storm of applause, the old man walked to the front and sat down at the desk. The orderly went over and poured him a cup of green tea. The room grew quiet as over one hundred pairs of eyers were fixed on Liu's sallow, wrinkled face.

"Sons," Liu said, "Little Si Ma wanted me to talk to you boys about the Long March. All right, I agreed. So I came. Now, let me first tell you how I joined the Red Army. It was in the spring of 1935, when I was seventeen. The Red Army came to my hometown, Mingyi, and took all the land from the landlords, and gave it to us poor folks. This means I wasn't in the Red Army when the Long March started, and I joined in when it passed our place."

The rustling of pens could be heard in the room. Si Ma wrote in his notebook, "Joined 1935, age 17."

Liu paused and looked at the swarm of dark heads. He resumed, "Why did I join the Red Army? Well, 'cause I could have something to eat. Dad and I went into the mountains to carry down firewood and sold it in town. The work was hard, and we never had enough food and clothes. Then the Red Army came. They caught the rich men and let the poor folks share out their wealth and land. Good, those parasites had to be wiped out. At long last, we, the oppressed men and women, could straighten up our spines and let out our anger. We took those fat landlords to a riverside and stoned them to death one by one. I was convinced that the Reds were our poor folks' army, so I joined in. For the first time, I had enough warm rice in my stomach and new clothes on my body. Two weeks later, I left home with the Red Army, for good."

Liu paused and looked rather vacant. "What should I talk about next, Little Si Ma?"

"Talk about the heroic deeds, like climbing the snow mountains and crossing the grass marshes." Si Ma was amused; he glanced at Commander Pei, who was gazing at Old Liu. Apparently Pei liked the old man and the way he talked.

"Oh yeah, the snow mountains," Liu resumed. "It was in the summer that year. We reached Baoshing, Szechwan Province, where the snow mountain is called Mount Jiajin. Nobody could see its peak, which disappeared in the clouds. When we set off, we didn't know it was all covered with snow. It was pretty warm at the foot of the mountain. In the beginning we even cracked jokes on the way, but after an hour, things changed. It began to snow, and then cold winds were howling. We had on only summer clothes. Oh, everybody began trembling with cold and fear. You could hear ghosts and spirits screaming on the mountain and in the black sky. I lost my sandals. They were no use anyway, 'cause my feet had to tread through the snow. Some men started to pray. They believed the mountain's spirits were angry at us. Then came a hailstorm. Oh heaven, those hailstones, as big as eggs, pounded us to the ground. One hit my forehead, and I was knocked down on my butt, my eyes filled with sparks and dark mists. Lots of men's faces were smashed and covered with blood, and some knelt down, kowtowing to the mountain peak. It didn't help. That was a spooky mountain; everybody believed so. In the end, we just buried our heads in the snow and let the hailstones strike our buttocks. The flesh is thicker there, more durable, you know. Ha-ha-ha!"

Some soldiers tittered. Si Ma turned around to stare at his men. Silence was restored.

"The grass marshes were no fun either," Old Liu continued. "People got stuck in the mud — the more you struggled to get out, the deeper you sank into it. You couldn't do a thing but watch your comrades sinking, and they disappeared right in front of you. I can't stand to recall it, and my stomach will ache again. Their screams were horrible; I can still hear them. We ate everything in the marshes — our shoes, clothes, waistbands, anything that water can boil. Chairman Mao had his horse shot and gave the meat to some sick men. Let's skip the marshes. I want to tell you something about the Tibetans. Any of you ever been to Tibet?"

"No," a dozen men said.

"We went there before the marshes. All the villages were deserted. We had no food, so we cut their barley to eat. But we paid them, put the money at the edges of their fields and used small stones to hold it down. The Tibetans didn't know that and thought we robbed them. They were barbarians and couldn't understand we were the people's army. So they deployed logs and rocks up on the hill waiting for us to pass the gorge in between. Once we entered it, they let everything roll down. My grandma! It was thundering on all sides, the logs rushing down on us, and the huge rocks smashing trees and anything in the way. We yelled and screamed and flung ourselves to the ground, and our horses jumped over our heads, running away. Every log finished off a dozen men; if you were not killed, you were scared half to death. I tell you, I couldn't get up from the ground; my legs had cramps. I was lucky and crept under a disabled horse cart — that saved my life. Oh those Tartars, I can never forget how fierce they were!"

Some soldiers put their hands to their mouths. A few laughed out loud. Si Ma stood up, his face red and hairy, which at once reminded the soldiers of his nickname, Monkey's Butt, so they couldn't help laughing some more. He said to Liu, "Old leader, tell us something about the battles and victories." He looked at Commander Pei, who gave him a meaningful smile and shook his round head.

"All right." The old man's eyes twinkled, and his sunken mouth jerked to the left. Taking a gulp of tea, he spoke again. "You've all heard of those victorious battles lots of times and must have calluses in your ears. Let me think of something else. Yes, here's one. How can I forget it? After Liupan Mountain, we arrived in a small town called Chuzhi, and we were putting up our tents for the night. All of a sudden, the enemy's cavalry came in the dark. We had walked for a whole day and had no strength left to fight. But the enemy and their horses were fresh; they'd been waiting for us for days. At once our troops burst out in every direction. We dashed around running for our lives. It was impossible to fight the enemy, and we had no horses and no time to deploy our men for a counterattack. I lost my head, just following those men in front of me. We jumped down a cliff that was not very deep. I lost my rifle there. Life was more important, so I didn't stop to retrieve it. I lost my cap too. We were just running and running. Then I vaulted over a small haystack and landed in a pigsty. My face hit a slanting pole, and my nose was bleeding."

Some men giggled. Secretary Si Ma stood up again. "Keep quiet and listen to the leader!" The giggling men lowered their heads and stopped.

Si Ma sat down. Do it to his mother! he cursed to himself. This old bugger talks like a counterrevolutionary.

"When I joined my company again," Old Liu went on, "they asked me where my gun was. I pointed to my bruised face and said, 'Look at my face.'

"But they said, 'We don't want to look at your face. We want to see your gun. Where is it?'

"'Gone,' I said, 'my gun's lost.' Our company commander ordered me to go back and recover it. How could I do that by myself? The enemy was in the town now. So I went away. Damn it, I thought, if you don't want your granddad in your unit, fine, I won't stay, so I took off. I had no idea how to return home and just wandered to the east, where I was told there was a big city. But on the way I ran into a medical team of the Red Army. They asked me, 'Little Comrade, why are you traveling alone?' I told them I'd had trouble with my leaders and the company wouldn't keep me anymore. 'Can you take me with you?' I asked.

"'All right, you can come on our nursing staff,' they told me, so I joined the Red Army again. This time I carried not a gun but a large chamber pot."

The entire audience burst into laughter, but the old man didn't even smile. He was gazing at the young faces calmly.

Secretary Si Ma got up again and waved to his men. He was sweating all over, and one of his molars was aching. "Comrades, be serious! We are in a lecture about the Party's history now." He turned to the old man, an awkward smile across his face, but he didn't know what to say. He'd heard that even the divisional leaders couldn't do anything about Old Liu when he got angry and swore at them, because none of them had joined the Red Army earlier than he had.

"But I didn't stay on the medical team for long," Liu resumed. "What happened was that the next summer, we wiped out two regiments of Chiang Kai-shek's troops and captured hundreds of prisoners. Among them there was an officer who was totally reactionary. Whenever we treated his wounds, he'd curse us. He called us 'Communist Bandits' and 'Red Beasts.' Everybody was outraged.

"One night after duty, I went to the kitchen to fetch water. A group of the leaders were eating and drinking in there. They all got drunk. Seeing me come in, Mess Officer Wan Fumin stopped me and said, 'Swig wine, Little Liu?'

"I took a gulp from his bowl. 'Eat meat,' he said, pointing to the plates on the table.

"'What meat is this?' I asked. We hadn't had any meat for months, and at the word *meat* my mouth began watering. They all laughed. 'Man meat,' Feng Shun said. He was the leader of the Guards Platoon. I was shocked and couldn't tell if he was serious.

"'You know that filthy-mouthed officer? This is his heart and liver, fried,' Wan told me, and picked up a chunk of the meat and put it in his mouth. He was chewing. I began to tremble and wanted to escape. But Wan handed me his chopsticks and ordered, 'Little Liu, try a piece. See if it tastes like mutton. You must learn to eat our enemy!'

"They all shouted to egg me on. I dropped the chopsticks and rushed out. I ran along the hilly road till the kitchen's candlelight disappeared behind me. The night was wet and cold. I sat in a millet field and dared not return before they went to bed. I wasn't sure if I should report them to the higher-ups. Who knew what was really going on? Perhaps the other leaders and medical officers had all accepted it as a custom to eat the enemies. Perhaps they had also shared the same sort of human dishes.

"The next morning, Wan and Feng grabbed me in our bedroom and said I mustn't be softhearted. Feng Shun said, 'If you feel pity for that mangy dog, you've confused an enemy with a friend. The love for our friends must be expressed in the hatred for our enemies. You mustn't take an enemy as a man!' I didn't understand what he meant exactly. I was scared, and my heart was shaking. What would happen if they took me as their enemy someday? Wouldn't they gobble down my insides too? So I made off again."

The room was so quiet that only Old Liu's breathing could be heard. Si Ma stood up and walked to Liu.

"I was not a deserter!" the old man yelled, pounding the desk with his small fists. Tears trickled down his cheeks. "I hate Chiang Kai-shek and all the reactionaries, but I dare not eat them! All right, I can kill them, but I can't eat their flesh. It's true I don't have the guts, but I'm not a deserter!"

"Calm down, please," Si Ma said and patted Liu's shoulder. He gestured for help. Three men in the front jumped up and went over. "Old leader, you're too tired," the secretary murmured. "You need a rest."

Two men helped Old Liu to his feet and supported him out of the room.

"Comrades," Si Ma addressed his men, "if you have taken some notes, you must tear the pages out and turn them in. Put them here." He brought his hand down on the desk. "Whether Old Liu's words are true or not is not our business to judge. What I want you to do is keep your mouths shut about this lecture. Liu is a Red Army man; something he says may not hurt him, but if you blab it out, you will be turned into a Current Counterrevolutionary. Do you understand?"

"Yes sir," they said in unison.

The room was at once filled with the noise of moving chairs. The soldiers were going to the front and placing their notes on the desk.

Commander Pei didn't move; he just sat there smoking a cigarette. His eyes were narrowed to short curves, squinting at the secretary time and again.

Si Ma was wondering why Pei wouldn't turn in his notes. Then it came to him that Pei had something against him now. He would have to write a report to the Divisional Political Department without delay, in case Pei informed the superiors of this lecture before he did.

The Russian Prisoner

Squad Leader Shi Hsiang returned from the Company Headquarters with eleven pistols and told us to pack up. Only summer clothes were needed, and everybody had to take his mosquito net. "This time we got an easy job," he assured us. Because we had the pistols, we left our rifles and submachine guns at our billet.

Twenty minutes later, we stood at attention facing Company Commander Yan Li in the middle of the drill ground. He called, "At ease!" and then described the "easy job." A fly landed on my cheek, crawling zigzag down to my chin. I dared not shake it off. Some piglets suddenly started screaming from the pigpens about fifty meters behind us. Squad Leader Shi told Wang Min to go tell Swineherd Liu to stop catching and gelding those piglets for a short while.

"This time," Commander Yan continued, "you Ninth Squad represent our company, undertaking the important task, directly under the command of Chief of Staff Shun. The Party and the people trust you. I hope everybody keeps in mind that anything you do will bear on the honor of our Guards Company. To guard the Russian prisoner is both a military task and a political task. You must not forget that to the Russian you stand for China and the Chinese Army.

You must show him our true revolutionary spirit. As I said just now, in appearance you should be polite to the Russian Big Nose and not give him the impression that he is a prisoner, because at this moment we don't know who he really is. But never forget it's our duty to keep him always under watch, day and night. Comrades, is that clear?"

"Yes sir," we shouted in one voice, clapping our heels together.

A new Liberation truck arrived. We climbed into it and sat down on our blanket rolls against the panels. As we were pulling out, the piglets began to squeal again. Off along a sandy road, the truck sped to the eastern outskirts of Longmen City. The scorching sun made us feel sleepy as we were tossed about in the truck.

Having left behind a long dragon of dust, we arrived at the Eastern Airport, a deserted military base built by the Japanese during the Second World War. Three young officers were already there waiting for us. Two of them wore cameras around their necks, and the other held a morocco briefcase. Everything had been arranged: Our room was upstairs in the small black-brick building, which was the only building at the airport; our dining room was on the first floor; the Russian captive and his Chinese interpreter would live in the two small rooms adjoining our large room, so that they had to cross ours to get out. There was also a recreation room on the first floor, and the Ping-Pong table looked brand-new.

"For the time being, treat him as a kind of guest. I mean in appearance," a tall officer with a gleaming gold tooth told our squad leader, while the rest of us were busy adjusting straw mattresses on the plank bed that stretched for fifteen meters across the large room. He was a staff officer from the Office of Tactics in the Divisional Staff, famous for his graceful handwriting. People called him Scholar Wang.

We all felt we could have a good time here. Everything seemed neat. At least we could avoid the summer drill.

Around three o'clock in the afternoon two Beijing jeeps pulled up in the center of the basketball court in front of the building. Divisional Chief of Staff Shun Hsin, his bodyguard, four officers, and the Russian captive got out of the jeeps. The Russian looked rather boyish and must have been under twenty-five. To our surprise, he was not as tall and big as we had expected, but just about as tall as most of the Chinese walking beside him, even shorter than Scholar Wang by half a head. He wore the Russian uniform; unlike ours, his cap had a big, broad peak. We watched attentively from upstairs, keeping our faces away from the windowpanes so that those outside would not notice us.

"He looks smart in that uniform," Wang Min said. "It must be made of wool."

"Gunnysack rags," Squad Leader Shi said. "It looks good only when it's new. You'll see how soon it will fall apart."

"His nose is not big at all," Ma Lin said.

"Why is his face so white?" Meng Dong asked.

"He must have drunk too much milk," Wang Min answered. "You see how large his round eyes are. That means he stuffs himself every day." Wang always liked to tease.

"Who's that old fellow with a gray goatee?" Vice Squad Leader Hsu Jiasu asked, referring to the officer who was walking between the Russian and the chief of staff, speaking to one and then the other.

"That must be Interpreter Zhang. He speaks Russian best in the province. Haven't you heard of Big-Beard Zhang?" the squad leader asked.

"No. He has no big beard."

"He used to have a long beard."

"The Russian doesn't look like an officer," I said.

"No, you're right, Song Ming," the vice squad leader

agreed. "He must be a soldier like us. Seems too young to carry bars and stars."

At this moment, one officer took out a shiny toylike machine gun and a green walkie-talkie from the back of a jeep and handed them to the two officers waiting with cameras, who brought them immediately into the building to take photos. Those items must have been the most advanced Russian equipment. The walkie-talkie looked like a lunchbox. None of us could tell what model the machine gun was, because our handbook of Russian weapons did not give a picture of it.

There were two extra rooms downstairs, which we were told not to enter. In the morning the officers would use the rooms when they interrogated the Russian captive. In the afternoon he was free, so we had to "accompany" him.

Toward evening, another jeep came and brought over Chef Wang, who worked in Longmen City's Guest Hotel. We heard that he was one of the best cooks in the province, and that his French cuisine had been highly appreciated by Premier Zhou Enlai. Certainly we had to eat our sorghum and rice, but we felt that eventually we might be able to take a bite of something unusual, since we had such an important "guest" among us. We enjoyed smelling the fragrance of the dishes prepared for the foreigner, which soon filled the first floor and the stairwell.

The Russian was called Lev Petrovich. According to his own account, he was a new soldier who had just arrived at the border. He used to serve as an orderly at the Headquarters of the Far East Military Region. Because of being lazy, he was sent to the Siberian border. That is what he said. It troubled us. We could not decide who he actually was and the true reason why he had crossed the border. Was he really a new soldier? Or was he an experienced agent? Did he come over to get information? Whom did he plan to meet? Or was it true as he said that the older soldiers forced him to carry both the machine gun and the walkie-talkie during their patrol along the border and that they deliberately gave him a hard time — not waiting for him when he was moving his bowels in the bushes — so he went astray and wandered onto our side? A group of peasants working in a hemp field saw him from far away. They deployed themselves as a trap. As soon as he entered the "bag," they jumped out, raising sickles, stones, hoes, and rifles, shouting: "Put down your weapon and we'll spare your life!" Lev didn't fight and just gave them his gun. This again puzzled us. It looked as though everything had been planned — he didn't even try to escape. Those officers questioned him every morning and didn't believe whatever he told them.

Chief of Staff Shun came to the interrogation for the first few days. Then Lev was left completely in the officers' hands. Our squad's major task was to stand the night guard. It was not a big thing, since each of us only had to stay awake for one hour in the hall. We didn't have to stroll around outside in the dark. In the morning we did nothing about him, so we studied the *Manifesto of the Communist Party* for two hours. In the afternoon, after two hours' nap, we played games with him if he wanted. He didn't join us very often in the beginning and read by himself a lot. Interpreter Zhang kept him company most of the time, because we couldn't make out what he babbled. They slept in the same room, where two mosquito nets hung on either side of the window, whose opening was blocked by six iron bars. Mr. Zhang had many of his books sent over, and the other small room was used as their study. I had never seen so many books, which filled four tall bookcases standing against the walls. Many of the bricklike books had pictures on their spines. Those were the portraits of Russian authors, some of whom had a big beard similar to Marx's or Engels's. We were awed by Mr. Zhang's books. We had heard that his father had been a general in Warlord Zhang Zuolin's army, and that his wet nurse was a Russian woman, so he could speak Russian fluently when he was a boy. But we hadn't imagined the interpreter knowing all those books. What a wise old gentleman. In fact, he was not so old, about forty-five, I think. Only his skin shriveled around his slender bones, and his narrow eyes looked bleary behind the thick glasses.

Sure enough, those books impressed Lev too. During the first two weeks, he always stayed in the study, reading and writing. We didn't expect him to be such a bookworm and also a lover of poetry. One early morning, we returned from our exercises and heard Lev shouting madly on the second floor. Hurrying upstairs, we ran into Interpreter Zhang in the corridor.

"What's the matter with him?" Squad Leader Shi asked.

"Nothing is wrong," Mr. Zhang said. "He's reading out Pushkin."

The door of the study was open. Holding a large book in his hands, Lev was yelling at the bright dawn beyond the window. His face looked sweaty and burning hot. Mr. Zhang went into the study and patted him on the shoulder. They talked and both sat down.

Soon we saw Mr. Zhang pacing up and down in the room with both hands in his trouser pockets, and we heard him humming Russian words, which must have been poetry, probably Pushkin's. Lev sat there stock-still, his eyes following Mr. Zhang and his large ears perked up. It was a long poem, for it took Mr. Zhang about ten minutes to finish. No sooner had he stopped than Lev got up and embraced his interpreter, murmuring something to him. Then we saw Lev pull a handkerchief out of his pocket and wipe his eyes with it. Mr. Zhang smiled, looking amused. We all thought it funny: Lev was like a woman, who would cry for beautiful words.

As our squad leader had predicted, Lev's uniform did look like gunnysack rags after a few washes. Now he wore our Dacron uniform, but without the red badges on his collar and the red star on his cap. Though he asked for a pair of badges and a cap insignia, the officers refused him. They said it was too soon for him to switch sides. As a matter of fact, he had thrown away all his Russian stuff, including the clumsy boots and foot wrappings, and instead he wore our green sneakers and cotton socks. It was funny that you could easily take him for one of us if you looked at him from behind. Once Vice Squad Leader Hsu tapped Lev on the neck, believing he was Wang Min, and said, "When will you buy us the Popsicles you promised?" Lev turned around, his gray eyes glittering with bewilderment, and his square, whiskered face broke into a feline grin. The large wart on his upper lip merged with his left nostril. Hsu was struck dumb. We all laughed and shouted: "Popsicles, five *fen* apiece," just as the old women vendors did on the streets.

Lev was an arrogant son of a bitch as well. Because we had been treating him as a guest, he was spoiled. He only smoked the two most expensive kinds of cigarettes: Ginseng and Great China. The staff officer Scholar Wang once gave him some Peony cigarettes, but Lev, after trying one, refused to accept them. He only wanted the best of the Chinese and took his privileges for granted. Naturally, he didn't know how to respect his hosts. One day he even stood on his hands on the head of our plank bed for a good two minutes. Having landed on the floor, he waved and seemed to invite us to a gymnastic contest. None of us could do that. Perhaps in his eyes we were all clodhoppers and didn't know how to do gymnastics or read those fat books.

He was smart indeed. On his desk there was a thick pile of paper, about two hundred pages. Mr. Zhang said those were Lev's thoughts on Lenin's *State and Revolution.* But all his smartness only caused more trouble for himself. No one would believe that a common Russian soldier could write an article the length of a book and could use the horizontal bar like a professional athlete. The more you thought about him, the more he looked like a well-trained agent.

We had to find a way to beat him in gymnastics. Even our officers couldn't perform well on the horizontal bar, so the Divisional Staff sent over Doctor Cai, who had been on the gymnastics team at the Chinese University of Medical Science, to compete with Lev. Certainly Lev was not Doctor Cai's match. The doctor's body was so lean and his muscles resembled those of a hound, whereas Lev's body looked powerful indeed but was too thick to be maneuvered deftly.

Behind the building Mr. Zhang introduced them, and they shook hands. Lev grabbed up some sand from the long-jump pit and ground it between his palms. Then he dashed forward, jumped up, held the bar, and flew back and forth in the air. Soon his body began circling around. We were all impressed, not having expected he could do the grand circles. He was flying around and around until his body slowed and stood still upside down on the bar. We were so surprised, we held our breath. After about five seconds, he swung down and landed on the ground. We clapped our hands reluctantly while he was smiling at us, breathing hard. Mr. Zhang handed him a towel.

Doctor Cai didn't bother to wipe his hands with sand. He walked calmly to the bar and hopped a bit to grab it. After remaining motionless for a few seconds, he started to move. Without doubt, our doctor was superior. In no time his body began flying in the same kind of grand circles. After five rounds, he suddenly let both hands go and swiftly flipped his body into a backward somersault. Coming down, he seized the bar again. We whooped, cheering him on. He repeated the same movement three times. Then he came to a handstand in the air. Gracefully releasing his left hand, he stood upright on only one hand. We all applauded and shouted "Bravo!"

The game was over. Lev, with a red face, went to the doctor and they shook hands again. He didn't look happy. It was good for him to understand that we Chinese were not so stupid as he thought, and that we could do whatever he did. For two days, he remained rather quiet and dared not challenge us.

But we all agreed he was a smart fellow who learned things fast. When he had arrived he could not play Ping-Pong; within four weeks he played as well as the best of us. It was so annoying that he always demanded you compete with him. He would point his Ping-Pong paddle at his chest and say: "Russia," and then at you: "China." Those were the first two Chinese words he could speak. He meant that each player represented his own country in the game. It made you nervous and unable to play at your best. Once he beat me — 21 to 18. I felt so bad that I could have torn him apart, but he was happy and gave me a Ginseng cigarette.

Even worse, after six weeks he could play Chinese chess (which he must never have seen before) better than any of us. And he always wanted to play it in the Russia-versus-China way. None of us dared play chess with him anymore, so we started to play poker, because in this game he had to choose one or more partners and could not represent Russia himself.

One afternoon we played One Hundred Points with him. His team seemed to be winning. He dashed the diamond king to the table and said loudly in Chinese, "Fuck you!" His doggy eyes turned around, looking at us seriously.

We were shocked, but then we all burst out laughing, and he laughed too. He didn't know what those words meant. From that day on, he began to use bad language in poker games. At first, we found it hilarious hearing him toss out those expressions, which we couldn't help using among ourselves. Then we began to worry. This meant that now he could understand some words in our language, and that he was trying to learn Chinese secretly. Scholar Wang told us to speak as little as possible when we played together. It was in our own interest not to let him understand us. He was our prisoner; if he understood our minds, God knew what would happen. So before long we played poker silently.

When he could not bear the silence, he would take out his wallet and look at the photograph of a girl, who he said was his girlfriend. He would kiss her right in our presence and then shamelessly grin at us, revealing his broad front teeth; or he would press her against his ear as if listening to her talk. By now he had got used to missing the girl. In the beginning, he had often gone to bed very early because he had missed her. We were convinced that the Russians were not good fighters. If you always thought of women, how could you fight? We all saw the girl's picture and agreed she was pretty in a way: yellow hair, gray eyes, peach-colored cheeks, and as slim as a sleek cat. She indeed looked different from other Russian women, who had breasts as large as basketballs. I was curious to see if Lev had pictures of naked women, because we had been told that every Russian soldier had at least five naked women in his wallet. But I didn't see any. It seemed Lev had only his girlfriend's picture with him.

Lev's immediate purpose for learning our language was to make out his whereabouts. Though he had been at the Eastern Airport for six weeks, he had no idea where he was. They had captured him in Hutou, which was merely two hundred *li* from Longmen, but they drove him in a jeep for a whole night from Hutou to Longmen, circling around and around the same mountains and back and forth through the same small towns. The windows on both sides of the jeep were covered with curtains; nobody but the Lord of Heaven could keep his bearings. Later Lev asked those officers about his location, and they refused to tell him. They also ordered us not to reveal to him what city we were in. He asked us many times and even drew a map on a sheet of paper, putting on it some Chinese cities he knew of, including Beijing, but we never identified the city we stayed in. The reason was very simple: If he had known his geographical location, it would have been easy for him to get in touch with some Russian secret agents.

Though we were still uncertain of who he was, his eagerness to find out where he was further convinced us that he was not merely a soldier. In addition to that, the Russians showed unusual interest in his case. They had continually asked about him and even offered to release some information on two Chinese defectors in exchange for information on him. Our side turned them down and refused to talk about Lev. Why was he so important to them? Of course we would not let them know anything about him before we could determine who he really was and decide how to handle him according to his true worth.

One evening, the men of our squad had gone to a movie shown at the Divisional Headquarters, and only Squad Leader Shi, Ma Lin, and I stayed with Lev at home. As usual, we played poker. Interpreter Zhang never joined us and always read in the study by himself. Lev took from his pocket a box of wine candies that Scholar Wang had given him; they contained the best wines. He put it on the table and made a gesture inviting everybody to share the dessert. We three looked at one another. Though a little surprised by his generosity, we didn't care much and just went ahead enjoying the candies. Shi picked up a maotai, Ma a five grains' sap, and I a green bamboo leaves. These were Chinese wines contained in Chinese candies, and our country provided Lev with them; since we were the hosts, why shouldn't we savor them?

After playing a few rounds, Lev stood up and moved to the door. Our squad leader gave me a hint with his eyes, and I immediately went out too. Lev walked into the lavatory. I followed him in, urinating and observing him at the same time. The window of the bathroom looked onto a vast cornfield. The moon was like a little boat anchored to a golden bank of clouds. After making sure he squatted down, I went out and waited in the hall. Five minutes later he came out. He moved close to me, looking mysterious. He took out a packet of Ginseng cigarettes and handed it to me. He put on a false smile and drawled in a nasal twang, "Changchun, Harbin, Jilin, Shenyang, Beijing?" He wanted me to tell him in which of these cities we stayed. His eyes were shining like a leopard's in the dark. I pushed aside his cigarettes and shook my head. He didn't mention Longmen and must have thought we were at least a thousand *li* away from Russia. That night he seemed rather absentminded during the game.

One thing we all liked about the guarding job was that we could have some good food. In the beginning Chef Wang cooked a lot of grand dishes for Lev. Only Interpreter Zhang ate with him, and he explained to him the names of the dishes and the ways they were made. Certainly Lev had never tasted anything genuinely Chinese. If he liked a dish on the first try, he would eat it all without touching the other six or seven dishes. Wiping out the first one, he would move to attack the second, then the third, and then, if he still had room in his stomach, the fourth. Through the crack between the door and its frame, we saw Interpreter Zhang watching him amusedly in the dining room, and we all laughed at his barbarous manners.

During the first week, at every meal Lev left some dishes untouched, so we, eating after him, would have those dishes in addition to our stewed vegetables and sorghum or rice. Oh, I had never tasted things so good! The quails, the bear palms, the frog legs, the oysters, the salmon, everything seemed eager to jump into your mouth. But we had to be patient, since we would share the dishes. Officers and soldiers were equal, just as we were all brothers. Chef Wang was really a kind old man, and he would smile watching us gobble down everything he made. Probably, he sometimes cooked a lot for Lev on purpose so that we could have more untouched leftovers.

As there were more important people to be fed, Chef Wang couldn't stay long to cook for Lev. There was no sense in treating an obscure Russian man like a state guest for good. In the beginning we fed him so well in hopes that he would cooperate and tell the officers whatever they wanted to know. He talked a lot indeed, and Scholar Wang always wrote down his words translated by Interpreter Zhang, but they could not figure out the credibility and value of what he said. So after three weeks Chef Wang left, and a cook was dispatched from the Divisional Headquarters. Though the new chef, Old Bi, did not cook as well as Chef Wang, he was good enough for Lev. Lev's daily meal expenses remained seven *yuan*, while every one of us had only fifty-five *fen* a day. In terms of board expenses, Lev ate more than our whole squad. There was no way he could eat so much, so we still benefited from his leftovers. However, Lev was civilized now — he would first try everything, make a plan of operation, and then launch an all-out attack.

One day after lunch Lev came out of the dining room with

a chicken leg in his hand. Mr. Zhang followed him, climbing the stairs while Lev kept chewing the meat. Passing a window in the hall, Lev threw the unfinished chicken leg outside. The interpreter saw it and started yelling at him in Russian. We didn't understand what he said, but we could tell he was very angry. None of us could imagine such a quiet, kind man could go mad like that. After they were in their room, we still heard Mr. Zhang shouting. He thumped the table again and again. A few minutes later, Mr. Zhang came out, walking quickly across our large room, and went downstairs. In no time he returned with a pair of chopsticks and a bowl of cooked sorghum partly covered with stewed eggplant, which was our lunch. He hurried past us, panting hard, his thick goatee vibrating a little. After he entered their room, we heard the chopsticks striking the table. Immediately we gathered at their door, peeping at them through the cracks in the plank.

Lev sat on the edge of his bed, hanging his head low. His face was as purple as an eggplant. Mr. Zhang raised the bowl of sorghum to Lev's face, and Lev turned his head away. Then Mr. Zhang went on talking loudly. It seemed he was teaching Lev a lesson — not to forget who he was, and to understand that some Chinese didn't even have sorghum to eat. He took up the bowl and began to eat the food himself while continuing to talk to Lev. We never found out what he said. Our squad leader asked Mr. Zhang afterwards, but he was told to forget about it.

More than being respectful, Lev was sort of attached to his interpreter. Three weeks after Mr. Zhang had yelled at him, a Russian gunboat was sunk by the Chinese militia in Hutou. The Russians protested, and a border negotiation was arranged. Mr. Zhang was summoned to join the delegation as the interpreter. During his absence, a young interpreter named Jiao Mu, a recent graduate from Jilin Foreign

Language School, came to accompany Lev. Lev seemed deliberately to make things difficult for Interpreter Jiao, pretending he didn't understand Jiao's Russian and constantly mentioning Mr. Zhang. Perhaps he meant to remind the young officer that he would never be as good as his predecessor. He even showed us how he missed Mr. Zhang — slapping his chest, saying "Zhang," and jerking up his square thumb.

Every day Interpreter Jiao reported to Scholar Wang that Lev had asked when Mr. Zhang would be back, as though Lev had felt something ominous. It turned out that Mr. Zhang would never be back with him again. He died in Hutou right after the negotiation. When he had arrived at the county town, he felt a pain in his stomach, but he didn't take it seriously; he just took some painkillers and set out with the delegation. Once they were in Russia, the pain grew intense. Because he was the only interpreter in our delegation, he had to be present at the talks, which were to last for a whole day with only a lunch break. During the morning negotiation, he swallowed one tablet after another and tried hard to interpret the dialogue. He came out of the hall sweating all over. While the other officers were having lunch, he lay on a sofa unable to move. The Russians sent for a doctor. The diagnosis was acute appendicitis, and Mr. Zhang needed an immediate operation. But the negotiations were to continue in the afternoon. Without our own interpreter, the talks would be controlled by the Russians and they would cheat us, and we might make some agreements in their favor, so Mr. Zhang struggled to his feet and worked until the meeting ended. Now the doctor said the patient must be operated upon, with absolutely no delay. The Russians offered to have Mr. Zhang taken to their hospital and after the operation they would send him back. Our chief delegate, Commissar Lin of our division, asked Mr. Zhang if he wanted to stay in Russia for a few days. Mr. Zhang refused, saying with tears in his eyes: "I will never have my illness cured . . . by our enemy. If I'm dying, please, please let me die in our Motherland!" So they drove him back to Hutou as fast as they could, but they stopped on the way again and again, finding the road flooded and two bridges washed away by mountain torrents. Desperate as they were, they couldn't get to the headquarters of the Fifth Regiment until three in the morning. It was too late, and Mr. Zhang passed away.

He became our hero. The Political Department of Shenyang Military Region issued a general order that required all officers and soldiers to study Zhang Fan's moving deeds and learn from his love for the Motherland and his unbreakable Chinese spirit. The newspaper *Forwards* described his life and his last moments in a full front-page article. When we read the paper, we couldn't control our tears. He was awarded the First Class Merit Citation, and the Zhangs became a Revolutionary Martyr's Family.

Though we all felt terrible about his death, none of us took it harder than Lev. Now he had to depend on Interpreter Jiao to translate Mr. Zhang's story in the newspaper. The young interpreter spent a whole evening in the study putting the article into Russian. The next morning after breakfast, Lev read the article, and he cried loudly, as though his parents were dead. The whole building could hear him. He wailed for almost an hour. In fact, he later told Interpreter Jiao that Mr. Zhang had been like a father to him and had taught him a profound patriotic lesson. We had never thought Lev had a heart. That day he didn't eat lunch.

After that Lev picked up a strange habit — whatever was Russian had to be good and better and the best: Russian weather was the most congenial, Russian girls the most pretty, Russian horses the most powerful, Russian pigs the most delicious, Russian apples the most juicy, Russian tongues the most clever.

We didn't bother to argue with him whenever Mr. Jiao interpreted to us what he said, except that once Wang Min challenged him to pronounce a few Chinese sounds that Lev's clumsy Russian tongue couldn't manage. We laughed but then agreed to let him indulge himself in his Russian chauvinistic dreams alone.

The officers all went home at night and slept with their wives. Interpreter Jiao took over the night command. He had been an officer for just three months and had not yet dropped the airs of a college student. Not used to acting as a superior, he would not demand to have more men if we left him only two men guarding Lev in the evening when the rest of us went to a movie or a game in Longmen City. Three people together with Lev could play any kind of poker game. Unlike Mr. Zhang, Jiao would join in whenever Lev played with us. He wanted to seize every opportunity to improve his Russian. He was the root of our troubles; after he came, our vigilance slackened little by little.

On a Tuesday evening, we all went to the Divisional Headquarters to see a movie, having left Vice Squad Leader Hsu and Wang Min with Interpreter Jiao at home. We heard that it was an anti-espionage movie made by North Korea, and everybody felt excited. No sooner was the title, *The Invisible Front*, shown on the screen than the lights were on again. The loudspeaker announced: "Emergency call, emergency call: All officers and soldiers leave immediately and gather outside.

"Emergency call, emergency call . . ."

We jumped up and ran out. In front of the movie house we joined our company. Commander Yan was walking to and fro before us with his hands behind him, waiting for more men to arrive. The whole yard was full of shouts: "Engineer Battalion —" "Communication Battalion gather here —" "Antichemical Company go to the gate."

Our political instructor Niu shouted to the crowd rushing out of the movie house, "Here's Guards Company."

Commander Yan called for attention, and we pulled our feet together. "Number One has escaped," he declared.

I shuddered. "Number One" was Lev — our first Russian prisoner. The commander continued, "The orders just came from Beijing: We must mobilize all the troops and the militia in Longmen and the neighboring cities and counties to search every field, every hill, every ditch, every yard, every cellar until we catch him. Now, we've no time to decide who is responsible for his escape. It happened in our company, and it's our responsibility to bring him back. The divisional leaders have ordered us not to return until we find him." He paused, then shouted: "Right face. Double time."

We actually sprinted back to our company barracks to get guns. Running in front of me, Squad Leader Shi never stopped cursing Vice Squad Leader Hsu and Wang Min. "Damn it, I'll do the two asses in! They ruined us all. I'll finish them off!"

Our company got on four trucks and were driven to the Eastern Airport. On the way we saw lights on in all the other barracks and heard people shouting and trucks moving everywhere. The entire city was going into action. Our trucks were running at full speed. Mosquitoes and moths struck our faces while Platoon Leader Fang, clutching the panel of the truck, was busy dividing us into groups. Each group had three men who were to stay together in the search.

The trucks pulled up in front of the building at the airport. We jumped down. Interpreter Jiao, Hsu Jiasu, and Wang Min ran over. Shi clutched the vice squad leader's upper arm and cursed, "Screw your ancestors! You undid us all!"

"Old Shi, listen to me. Please listen —"

"Cut it out!" Platoon Leader Fang shouted. "Shi Hsiang, let him go. I said let go! You think you can get away with this? I tell you, you are the one responsible. If we can't bring Number One back, we'll all go home turning up dirt clods. Stop biting each other, man. Save your breath for the job. Hsu Jiasu, you go join the sixth group, and Wang Min, you go with the seventh group."

The two squad leaders stood among their groups motionless as Wang Min walked over to our group. "Remember," the platoon leader went on, "keep fifty meters between groups and don't move too fast."

We started to search. Meng Dong led our group, which included Wang Min and me. We walked slowly in a cornfield, trying hard to see if there was something hidden in the field's ditches. The corn leaves lashed our faces time and again, but we dared not complain. It was terrifying to make our way through the crops. The cornstalks were thick and taller than we were, and we couldn't see our neighboring groups. We only heard them proceeding quietly. The most frightening part was that we didn't know if Lev had a gun with him, though we had been told that he had not stolen any of our pistols. He was in the dark and could observe us moving. If we ran into him, surely he would shoot first. Full of fear, we used our rifles to remove the cornstalks in our way, always keeping the barrels pointed at the darkness ahead.

After combing the cornfield, we entered a soybean field. This was less frightening, since we could see other groups advancing with us in a line. Then we got into a cabbage field. God knows how many cabbages we trampled. Behind us the field was scarred with numerous dark tracks.

In front of us, two German shepherds, accompanied by some officers, were dashing in opposite directions along a brook. One of the dog handlers was carrying Lev's pillow, and the other was holding Lev's washbasin. They threw the pillow and the basin to the dogs time after time to refresh their memory of Lev's smell so that they could pick up his trail. There were six dogs all together, running about and barking, but none of them was any good. They ran in six directions, so the officers soon lost interest in them.

In the beginning we dared not talk. After crawling through four fields, Wang Min couldn't contain himself anymore and started cursing. We asked him how in the world the whole thing had happened. He said it was nobody's fault. Lev, the son of a wolf, wanted to make a fool of us on purpose:

"We were playing cards, and he said . . . he wanted to go to the bathroom. I went with him — Watch your step, Song Ming — I saw him squat down and — as usual, waited outside for him to finish. I waited for ten minutes, and he didn't come out. Interpreter Jiao . . . and Hsu Jiasu came to see what . . . was going on — Slow down a bit, Old Meng. We have to wait for the other groups — We three went in the bathroom. Lev was still squatting there, so we came back out. Then we heard a thump, and we went in again. Lev was not there! He had jumped out the window. We leaned on the window . . . and saw him down there staggering along . . . toward the cornfield.

"'Halt! Le-v, halt! Come back, Lev!' we shouted from upstairs. He didn't even turn his head, just walked straight ahead, and disappeared in the field. Interpreter Jiao didn't know what to do. He could only shout, 'Just look at that, just look at that!' Hsu Jiasu told him . . . to call the headquarters. Then we both ran out looking for Lev in the fields."

"Did you find him?" Meng Dong sounded rather serious.

"Damn you, Old Meng. You can still joke about it."

"You shouldn't have tried. It was impossible you two could get him back."

"You may be right, but we had to do it. It's a part of the job, you know."

"What will you do if we catch him?" I asked Wang Min.

"I'll make him drink horse pee!"

"I'll increase his meal expenses," Meng said. We all laughed.

"Hey, stop laughing, men," Ma Lin shouted at us. He was in the group on our left. "We're all going to the hill ahead and beat the woods."

We set out for the foot of the hillock. Lev's escape puzzled us. Did he plan to meet someone, an agent, at a certain place? Did he know in what direction Russia was? He must have known, otherwise what was the good of escaping? Did he have weapons and food with him? Why did he run away just a week before the National Day? Was he joining someone in order to destroy a factory or blow up a bridge on October 1? None of these questions could be answered. But one thing we were all certain about — if he knew his whereabouts, he would be able to return to Russia, because it was midfall now and the crops could cover him. Though more than thirty thousand troops and militia were in the operations, there was no way that we could go through every place in this vast area of eleven counties and three cities. Besides, he was a live creature and could move about to avoid us. More to his advantage was that he would not starve in the season of harvest, since there were fresh beans, corn, potatoes, and vegetables in the fields everywhere and even ripe fruits in the mountains. As long as he knew his bearings, he could get back to Russia. It seemed somebody among us must have accepted his bribery and told him that he was in Longmen. If Lev succeeded in hiding out or crossing the border, then everyone in our squad would be suspected. We had to bring him back to clear ourselves.

It was one o'clock now. We had been searching for almost five hours without rest. Whoever we came across, soldiers or militia, would curse "The Russian Big Nose," "The Polar Bear," "The Russian Hairy Beast." They didn't know Lev's name, or what he looked like. We dared not tell them, because he had broken loose from our hands. Also, Lev was really an egg of a turtle, deserving any name. We had treated him so well, but he betrayed us and made us crawl around on a dark night like this, hungry and exhausted.

We hadn't brought overcoats and food, nor could we go back and fetch them. The orders stated clearly: "Do not return until you find him." After five hours' walk, we were tired out and dying to eat something. There were edibles in the fields, but none of us dared touch them. The Second Rule for the Army says never take anything that belongs to the people, so we tried hard to stand the hunger and went on searching.

But we couldn't keep this up. It was cold. Dewdrops fell on us from the tops of the crops, and our clothes were soaked through. Without food in our stomachs, we felt as if our bones were hollow inside and couldn't help trembling.

We entered a turnip field where sorghum also grew. Between every dozen rows of turnips, there were four or five rows of sorghum. Every group was walking in its own turnip strip and couldn't see the other groups in the adjacent strips. Wang Min said, "Can't we have a tur-turnip?" His teeth were chattering.

"It's gnawing inside," I said, kneading my stomach.

"Why not?" Meng Dong kicked down a turnip. He tore off the leaves and began gobbling.

We all got our turnips. Wang Min stabbed the head of his turnip with his bayonet to get rid of the leaves. "Don't use the bayonet. It's poisonous," Meng warned him.

Wang was a new soldier and forgot that. He threw away the turnip and pulled up another one, as big as a baby. Soon we all stopped talking and ate quietly. We were afraid that the groups on both sides might know what we were doing, so we tried to make as few noises as possible. Who knew what they were doing? They might have been eating turnips too. People all at once fell into silence, and we only heard muffled footsteps advancing.

I finished the turnip and yanked up another. Meng got his second one too. Wang's was too big to finish. Thank God, the field was long, and I could eat up the second turnip before we got out of it.

Now it was two-thirty, and we were told to pull up and get two hours' sleep. Our company leaders must have thought that the search would last for days, so they didn't want to wear us out too soon. We all sat down on a flattish slope that separated a soybean field and an oak wood, but this time everybody stayed by himself and kept a distance of thirty meters from the next man.

Soon it became quiet, and only a few barking dogs could be heard vaguely. Stars hung loosely in the dark purple sky. Some streaks of clouds fluttered beneath the majestic silver moon, which laid its steely beams on the damp plants and the furrowed land. The stuff in my stomach started stirring and made me want something warm and hot, soup or porridge, which could relieve the uneasiness inside. Turnips were a good vegetable for opening bowels, and one turnip was more than enough for that purpose, but I had rammed two into my stomach. Now heartburn replaced hunger.

If only we had a fire and could roast some fresh soybeans . . . it's so cold . . . oh my knees . . . they are numb . . . not my own . . .

Peanuts, fresh peanuts, so delicious, just roasted . . . together with the vines . . . come sit here, close to the fire . . . what a good flat stone, warms up your feet so well . . . give me some room . . . I want to heat up my lunch — salted mackerel and corn cake . . . smells so good . . . the sun, what a spendid sun, dry and warm ... those clouds ... wonderful — horses and cows ... also apples and pears ... hah, we have everything here ... Fourth Dog, where's your brother ... call him to stop digging for potatoes ... don't be greedy ... the whole field is ours ... nobody knows this place ... Lilian, take a bite of this melon ... it will melt your teeth ... why laughing ... it's sweeter than anything from Dwarf Liu's garden ... hey, all of you ... come here ... peanuts, fresh peanuts roasted with vines ... don't you want to have some ... sit here around the fire and eat ... everybody is welcome ... today's Communism Day — take whatever you need ... why are you giggling, Old Meng ... don't you feel happy ... you son of a goat ... don't you want to have fun ... where's Lev ... he was eating peanuts here just now ... you mean he's taking a piss in the bushes ... hey, who's there ... is that you, Lev ... no, it's Wang Min ... Wang — Min — ... tell Lev we have baked sweet potatoes too ... more good eats for him to wipe out ... Ma Lin, give me your fur coat ... don't be selfish ... it's my turn to be warmed ... who is blowing a whistle there ... damn, who's the killjoy —

"Guards Company get up" ... who is yelling — "Guards Company get up."

I jumped to my feet and picked up my rifle. Kneading my arms, I felt numbing pains in the elbows. My knees went shaky too, and I slapped my legs to wake them up. What a dream! I had dreamed of so many good things, but everything was messed up. How could so many people get to one place — my home village? Terrible, I even dreamed that Lev was our friend. All gathered in Fox Valley.

Oh how I miss home! Home, the place that is always warm and safe, where you can sleep a whole day and a whole night when you're so dog tired. Mom will bring a bowl of millet porridge, hot and delicious, to the side of your pillow when you open your eyes in the morning, and there will be four poached eggs in the porridge. Oh Mom and Dad, how I miss you! —

My thoughts were interrupted by some people's swearing. They cursed Lev again, wishing him to be crushed to death and licked to a skeleton by bears.

It was almost dawn. A thin curtain of fog surrounded the oak woods and spread above the fields. Every blade of grass was heavy with dew. The air smelled grassy, but everybody seemed to lack the strength to breathe in the fresh air. We spread out along the slope quietly, forming a long line at the edge of the woods. I felt dizzy, and my forehead was still numb. A woodpecker was hammering at a tree trunk, and the sound seemed to shake the entire mountain as we started moving.

When we got out of the fog, suddenly the dawn was opening and the east turned pink and bright. Beneath the eastern sky, we saw people running down along a winding path on the hillside. Somebody guessed they must have caught Lev. Commander Yan raised his field glasses to watch while we were gathering around him.

"No," he said. "It looks like another injured militiaman. They're carrying a stretcher on their shoulders."

"This is not war yet," Platoon Leader Fang said, "but there's already a depletion of numbers."

"Attention, everybody." Commander Yan turned to us. "We are going ahead through the thicket in front of us now. When we're out of it, we'll have breakfast."

We set off again, thinking of warm porridge and steaming bread for breakfast. The night before it was reported that two militiamen had been injured. Some of the militia had forgotten to lock the safety catches on their guns.

The thicket was very small. Soon we sat down for breakfast, which was hardtack and cold water. The biscuits were not bad, but we'd like to have drunk some hot water, still shivering with cold. No fire was allowed, because the smoke might show Lev where we were. Though there had been no shadow of Lev, we had to act as if he was within our range.

After breakfast we rested for an hour. No one knew what place should be searched more thoroughly than anywhere else. Walking aimlessly like this, we could not find any trace of Lev, so it was better to take it easy.

At ten o'clock our squad was sent to search around a slaughterhouse in a valley. We were told not to wander far away, just stay within that area. By this time every pass and every juncture, from Longmen to Hutou and to the border, had been occupied by troops, militia, and villagers. Lev had already fallen into the boundless ocean of people's war.

Slowly we moved through the millet field east of the slaughterhouse. Everybody tried to relax a little while his legs were dragging him forward. The two squad leaders had already made up. It was always like that: They quarreled, looking as if a melee was about to break out, but an hour later they would become pals again. All of us were in a better mood now, except that everybody swore whenever Lev came to his mind.

The slaughterhouse butchered oxen in the daytime. After the first search through the millet and the soybean fields nearby, we went to the slaughter hall to see how they killed oxen. Ma Lin said that the folk in his hometown would trip the animal to the ground first, than stab its heart with a long knife, but Vice Squad Leader Hsu said, "Nonsense, you have to use a sledgehammer to knock out the ox first. Who can trip up an ox!"

We all went to see. In the large hall hung a few headless oxen that had been disemboweled but not yet skinned. Probably because it was lunchtime, there were only two men in there. One of them looked like a master and the other an apprentice. They nodded at us and didn't seem to mind our presence. The master was tall and stout. The flesh on his cheeks was thick and squeezed his eyes into two tiny triangles. The apprentice was also tall but thin and narrow shouldered. His big jaw had grown sideways, his chin almost in a vertical line with his left cheek. He looked brain-damaged. Wang Min asked them to show us how they butchered an ox, and they agreed. I was wondering how just the two of them could kill such a large animal.

They placed a piece of rope into a sort of groove on the floor, forming a chain of four nooses. A small knife, about five inches long, dangled on the master's hip. Then they went into the cattle pen behind a green gate and pulled in a large ox. The animal saw the carcasses in the air and refused to move forward. Around its shoulders there were hairless patches, so it must have done a lot of work. Its eyes looked dim. Tears, I saw tears rolling down its cheeks. The two men were pulling hard.

As soon as the ox's hooves were in the trap, they hauled at the ends of the rope. With a bang the ox fell to the floor. Its four legs were tied up struggling in the air. The young man hit its forehead with a sledgehammer, and the ox instantly stopped moving. The master jerked out the short knife and started cutting the ox's head. Beneath the blade whitish flesh flared and then turned ruddy. With three strokes the head was slashed off. The whole process took no more than twenty seconds. On the floor, a foamy crimson pool extended, and the hall at once filled with an odor of compost.

I walked away, my chest and stomach twinging inside. In front of me, small stars were jumping about on the wormwood. I felt like vomiting but could not bring anything up. They killed an ox like a chicken. Grandma was right: The most wicked creature on earth is man. That ox had worked for its master till it was old; when it couldn't work well, the master sold it to the slaughterhouse for money. The ox had wept just now, begging the fat butcher in silence for its life, but people wanted to eat beef, so they ignored its tears and butchered it. Man is a true beast.

When I rejoined my comrades at the edge of a soybean field, they were having a lunch break, still talking about the scene in the slaughter hall. Everybody had been impressed; nobody had expected that a big ox could be killed without any noise. Lunch was hardtack too. At breakfast each of us had been given two extra pieces for noon. I was hungry and forced myself to eat, but I felt sick and couldn't eat as fast as the others. Our squad leader told me to take my time. Meanwhile, those who had finished lunch lay on the grass, smoking tobacco.

The news came at three o'clock that Lev had been caught. Rejoining our company, our platoon took a truck to the Divisional Headquarters to wait for him. Everybody was talking about how to handle Lev once we had him in our hands again.

It turned out that Lev had never known what city he was in, nor had he been able to tell in what direction Russia was. All night he ran inland, but he covered only thirty *li*. He had been totally spoiled by us. Contrary to our fears, he simply couldn't eat anything in the fields. He had eaten too much of the delicate food and the best candies, and had smoked too many of the expensive cigarettes, so for a whole night he didn't eat anything, no matter how hungry he was. By noon he couldn't endure the hunger anymore; he got out of the cornfield where he had hidden himself, went over to an old peasant who was passing by, and asked him for food and cigarettes. The old man knew who he was, brought him home, and gave him a pipe, then told his wife to cook. In the meantime his daughter ran to the office of their production brigade to tell the militia. When the militiamen arrived, Lev was eating scallion cake, scrambled eggs, and bean sprouts. They surrounded the house but didn't disturb him. Then a jeep from Chaoyang County's Military Department came and picked him up.

Now we were ready to receive him. The militia, the police, and the people on the streets all knew we had recaptured the "Russian agent." Standing in two lines at the entrance of the Divisional Headquarters, we kept the militiamen and the people away from the front sentry post. Some of them carried guns and many held carrying poles and spades. They declared they wanted to teach the "Russian agent" an unforgettable lesson. Everyone was angry, having not slept for a night and having trudged around for twenty hours. Besides, so many crops had been trampled. Even some policemen said they wanted to beat the Big Nose too.

Our squad was told to accompany him back to the Eastern Airport. From now on, all the privileges Lev had enjoyed were taken away, and his daily meal expenses would be the same as ours. He was to eat with us.

Here came the jeep. The moment it stopped, Lev got out with a pair of handcuffs on his wrists. Some people were rushing to him. Lev could tell they wanted to beat him, so he hurried to us but then paused, probably noticing us all fully armed. We hated him — because of him we were notorious now, and every one of us would have to do self-criticism for several days.

Seeing the few men around him holding only carrying poles, we didn't seriously intervene but merely shouted, "Don't beat him. Don't use force." We thought a few strokes wouldn't hurt him much and would give him enough of a warning not to escape again.

"Ouch!" Lev slumped down and started screaming. His body spun around on the gravel road and fell into the roadside ditch. There he lay on his back, and the green uniform on him turned mottled. His arms circled his head, wriggling to loosen the handcuffs, while his legs stretched motionless.

"Halt, halt!" We all ran over and pushed the wild people away. We had not expected they would beat him as if they wanted to kill him. A young man was still struggling along in the crowd, waving a carrying pole in the air and crying, "Let me go! I'll get even with him, the Russian Tartar." He was the one who had broken Lev's right leg. We caught him, together with his pole, and brought him into the headquarters. Later we came to know that his elder brother, a platoon leader in the militia, had been shot by a carbine going off accidentally that morning.

Meanwhile Lev was moved into the Office of Mail and Information. He smelled like a goat, and his body was quivering on the cement floor. He was moaning in a choked voice and kept his eyes closed, as if he were a dumb animal that couldn't speak a human word, although Interpreter Jiao was standing by. Some parts of his clothes were soaked with sweat. Squad Leader Shi held up Lev's neck and raised a glass of cold water to his mouth. Lev drank it up without opening his eyes. It seemed he didn't care whether we gave him water or poison.

Doctor Cai came with an ambulance. We carried Lev out and put him into the van. Immediately the siren started and the ambulance sped to the Twenty-third Field Hospital.

That night we packed up and returned from the airport to our billet in the Company Headquarters. It was the last time we saw Lev, whose identity was clarified after his escape, since he had no one to meet and even fled toward Beijing to get back to Russia.

We were told two months later that he was returned to his country in exchange for a defector from the Fourth Regiment. Though we knew who Lev Petrovich was now, I guess, it would not be easy for him to prove who he was to the Russians. They would suspect him of being either a traitor or a Chinese agent. Lucky for him, he had a broken leg.

The Fellow Townsmen

After lunch I was lying on the bed and reading a novel, *The Boundless Snow and Forest*. Scribe Hsu Fang came in and said, "Instructor Chen, there's a man outside from your hometown. He wants to see you."

"Really, who is he? Are you sure he is my fellow townsman?" I got up and put the book on the bedside table.

"Yes, he said he wanted to see you."

I went out to the drill ground. The sun was scorching. The barracks were quiet since the men of my company were taking a nap.

Hmm, Chu Tian, of course he was my townsman. Although he wore civvies, I recognized him at first sight. If he had shed his skin and flesh, I could have identified his bones. Strange to say, he was carrying on his back a sleeping child, from whose gaping mouth was dripping a thread of saliva. He smiled at me awkwardly, his bony face stretching sideways and his cupped ears sticking out of unkempt hair.

"Why do you want to see me?" I asked, wondering how he had fallen into such a state. How did he come to be like a beggar, wearing blue rags and reeking of ram urine? He reminded me of a pig in a muddy pen.

"Chen Jun, I — I wouldn't trouble you, if I had a way out. My boy is sick, pneumonia, so we came to you for help." His thick nose twitched.

"Why me? Aren't you a doctor yourself?"

"I don't know anybody here but you. Please forget the hard feelings between us for the moment. He's dying. Save the child, please!"

What could I do? I led him into my room in the Company Headquarters and then sent for the medic, Ren Ming. The boy seemed very sick and hardly made any noise.

Ren told me we had plenty of penicillin. Being a doctor himself, Chu sterilized a syringe with a cotton ball and injected a large dose into his son's rump. He lay the boy on my bed. "There, there, have a good sleep." He covered him with a dirty jacket.

Damn, allowed into my room, he took my bed.

Chu turned to me. "The pneumonia was caused by measles. But as long as we have penicillin, I can cure him." He sighed. "We've traveled for over a month, sometime sleeping in train stations at night and sometimes in the open air. I'm lucky that I haven't fallen ill myself. He's too young to stand this kind of life."

I didn't make any comment, but his last few sentences aroused my interest. Scribe Hsu Fang brought in a thermos bottle and three mugs. He placed them on my desk and went out.

"I have a lot of things to do this afternoon," I said, ready to leave. "You can stay here with the boy."

As I was walking out, Chu stood up. The rascal, at least he didn't forget to be respectful here.

I don't know why I didn't tell him to go away, to get out of my face. I hated him. He had been engaged to my elder sister for three years and then jilted her because he had been promoted to officer's rank in the army. Certainly girls in Beijing were more attractive, with whiter faces and softer bodies, certainly he was no longer the country boy he had been, but it was immoral for him to throw away his fiancée simply because his status had improved. My sister wept for days, saying she could not go out and face others. I remembered that I had wanted to go to Chu Village, which is six *li* from ours, and ask his parents to give a good reason for his breach, but my mother stopped me, saying there was no use. The Chus were too powerful for us to quarrel with.

I hated his guts! But what should I do now? In the presence of my men, I could not be rude to him, especially after the sentry, the medic, the orderly, and the scribe had all seen the sick boy. Though reluctant to treat him as a fellow townsman, I told the mess squad to prepare a guest dinner for two. In the soldiers' eyes, it would be shameful to let your fellow townsman eat an ordinary meal. It seemed he wouldn't leave in hours, and I had to pay out of my own pocket for the dinner. Of course I didn't mind feeding him, but only with horse droppings.

How had he come to be living the life of a vagrant? What a dandy he had been six years before, when he returned home for the Spring Festival from Beijing, where he served as a doctor in the army's Central Hospital. Both his wife, a pharmacist, and he wore shiny leather shoes and brand-new green overcoats. When they walked on the street, children would follow them, whistling and shouting, "Big officers. Turn back. Big officers." At that time, I was merely a squad leader, and he didn't bother to nod his head when we passed each other in our town. Now look at him — even the dogs in his home village would growl at such a tramp.

Company Commander Yee was away with the Third Platoon in the Southern Mountains helping the peasants with their harvest, so I didn't invite anybody to dinner and sat alone with Chu in my room. The boy, still sleeping, was better, his temperature three degrees lower. Chu kept glancing at the pork ribs and the fried tofu on the table.

"Help yourself." I filled my own bowl with rice. I didn't share a cup of liquor with him. A good meal was more than enough.

He swallowed a large piece of tofu and took a mouthful of rice. "Oh, thank you, Brother Chen. I haven't had such food for five weeks."

Shut up! Who's your brother?

"Brother Chen." He started again, showing his big yellow teeth. "I'll never forget this. Oh, so delicious!" His lips were oily.

I didn't say a word, just ate. He sensed my resentment and kept quiet.

After two bowls, I asked him casually, "What's happened to you?"

He gave out a sigh, still chewing on a rib. "It's hard to explain in a few words."

"Tell me about it."

As I was making tea, he began his story. "Two months ago, at a cadre meeting, the commissar of our hospital asked us to make criticisms. Everybody was supposed to say something. When it was my turn, I stood up and spoke on behalf of the Senior Officer Ward, because I was the acting director."

"What did you say?" I put a mug of tea before him.

"Thanks. I said, 'Seven nurses in my ward complained to me that a few senior leaders had made a pass at them. One general ripped Nurse Wen's skirt last week. I don't want to mention his name here. This sort of thing happens again and again in our ward. Those senior officers are older revolutionaries, who should be a model for us of the younger generation. On top of that, they all have grandchildren. It's a shame for them to behave like that.'" He picked a tea leaf from the mug and took a sip.

I wanted to laugh. What a blockhead. But I asked, "Then what happened?"

"At the meeting, the commissar said he would look into this matter. Everything seemed all right. But a week later, all of a sudden, the walls at the front of the hospital were covered with big-character posters, calling me names and accusing me of spreading counterrevolutionary views. I was scared. This was a matter of life and death. I had seen with my own eyes Marshal Chen Yi being roughed up by the Red Guards. I was nobody; if I fell into the hands of the revolutionary masses in our hospital, it would be my end. Two days later, when we were eating lunch, our neighbor Mrs. Liu hurried in and said, 'Young Chu, run, quick! They're coming for you.' Then we heard footsteps thumping in the stairwell. It was impossible to escape through the door now. My wife is a coolheaded woman. She said. 'Take our child with you; they won't leave him alone.' So I carried this boy on my back and climbed across to the Lius' balcony. I heard them yelling at my wife in our home, and I sneaked out through the Lius' apartment. I went to the railroad station directly and took a train, which happened to come to the Northeast. That's why we're here now."

"You are lucky." I didn't know why I said that. "Do you have any relatives here?"

"No, I don't know anybody but you. We just roam around, sometimes taking a train and sometimes walking. In Changchun City I saw a notice with my picture on it. It said I was a counterrevolutionary criminal and must be brought to justice. I'm sorry, I don't mean to get you involved —"

Orderly Meng Hai came in and set about clearing the table. I gave Chu a Glory cigarette, which he lit and drew at as if sucking his mother's breast. The child woke up. I told Meng to leave a bowl of food. Seeing meat and rice, the boy seemed to forget his illness and started bolting the food down. "Daddy, zo goot," he mumbled with his mouth full. I noticed that, unlike his father, the boy had the round eyes which were typical among the Chus.

"Eat slowly, Dundun." Chu touched his son's forehead, then said to me, "He's much better. The medicine works."

As soon as the orderly went out, Chu resumed, "I really don't want to get you into trouble, but we can't go to a hospital, you know. We won't stay long. I'm grateful, Chen Jun."

"You can't stay here for long. This is not a safe place either. Fortunately, the company commander is not home tonight."

"I understand. We'll leave tomorrow morning. Could you do me a favor, my good brother?"

"What?"

"Please give me a syringe and some penicillin."

"I'll see what I can do."

Nothing could be easy between him and me. Now he was in my hands, and I would not give him a pleasant time. My mother hadn't been able to raise her head before the villagers when he broke the engagement. My sister could have eaten him alive.

That night I told the medic to wrap up the medicine and a syringe, but this didn't mean I would let Chu go as he pleased. In fact, lying in the company commander's bed, I was thinking if I should report Chu to the Divisional Political Department. Who knew whether what he had told me was true or not? He might have been a true reactionary. This was an opportunity to show my loyalty to the Party and also get even with the Chus. Two weeks before, I had heard that the Political Department was considering promoting me to vice chief of the Divisional Officer Section. A company political instructor about to be promoted directly to a rank equal to a battalion commander's, do you think I would just sit waiting for the big pie to fall into my mouth? No, I had to do something. What was more appropriate than turning in a counterrevolutionary?

How about the child? I wouldn't care a damn. The boy was a seed of the Chus and should share his father's fate. I wouldn't mind if they were both captured. Tomorrow the first thing I was going to do was call the Divisional Political Department.

I went to sleep with the plan in my head.

But the next morning I began to change my mind. One thing I had not taken into account was that, if they came to arrest Chu, they might not be able to take the child with them, because Chu would surely ask me to take care of the little monster. Probably he'd beg me to have the boy sent back to our hometown, to Chu Village. How could I refuse my fellow townsman in the presence of the officers and soldiers? The child could be anything but a reactionary. I had to figure out a proper way to handle this.

After breakfast they were ready to leave. I had no time to think out an adequate solution, which could please the higher-ups and at the same time keep myself free from blame for Chu's arrest. It seemed there was no chance of making the job clean. I went on scratching my scalp but could not come up with an idea.

Finally, when I followed them out with the medical package under my arm, I said to myself, All right, let the rascal slip through your fingers just this once. There will be another time.

At the entrance of our building, I gave him the medicine. His eyes turned watery when he saw it. "My good Brother Chen, you are our benefactor. We will never forget you. Come down, Dundun, kowtow to Uncle Chen." He put the dirty boy on the ground.

"No, it's not necessary." I picked the small monkey up and handed him back to his father. I didn't want him to make a show in front of Orderly Meng and Scribe Hsu. Then, Heaven knows what muddled my brain at that moment, I took two ten-*yuan* bills out of my wallet and handed them to Chu.

He accepted the money and said with tears in his eyes: "Our savior, as long as we live, we'll remember this!" He turned around and walked away with the child on his back. The chilly breeze was lifting their rumpled hair from behind, while dried leaves were scuttling about ahead of them.

I am not sure why I did that. Perhaps I wanted to show my men that I was generous, or perhaps I wanted that scoundrel to remain grateful.

My Best Soldier

I couldn't believe it when I saw that the photo sent over by the Regimental Political Department was Liu Fu's. How clumsy he looked in it: a submachine gun slanted before his chest; above his army fur hat, in the right corner, stretched a line of Chinese characters, DEFEND MY MOTHERLAND; his smile was still a country boy's, lacking the sternness of a soldier's face. He had been in my platoon for only about ten months. How could he, a new soldier, become a secret customer of Little White Fairy in Hutou Town so soon?

Our political instructor, the Party secretary of our company, interrupted my thought. "I've talked with him, and he admitted he had gone to that woman six times this year."

"Six times?" Again I was surprised. "He is new. How could he get to know her so quick?"

"I asked the same question." Instructor Chang tapped his cigarette lightly over an ashtray and raised his head, looking across the small room in which we were sitting. He wanted to make sure that the orderly was not in the next room. "I think there must have been a pimp, but Liu Fu insisted he got to know the Fairy by himself when he had his hair cut in her barbershop. Obviously he is a novice in this business. No old hand would leave his picture with that weasel."

"You're right." I remembered last year a bulletin issued by the Regimental Political Department had carried a report on this young woman. After being caught in bed with an officer, Little White Fairy was brought to the Regimental Headquarters, where she confessed many soldiers and officers had visited her. Once she had received six army men in a single night, but she didn't know any of their names. Each man gave her a two-*yuan* bill and then went to bed with her. That was all. Regimental Commissar Feng swore to have those men found out, for they must have belonged to our Fifth Regiment, the only army unit in Hutou. But those were old dogs who had never left any trace.

"You should talk to him." Secretary Chang exhaled a small cloud. "Comrade Wang Hu, your platoon has done everything well this year except this Liu Fu matter. Don't get lost in the training. Mind modeling is more important. You see whenever we slack a little in ideological education, problems will appear among our men."

"Secretary Chang, I'll talk to him immediately. From now on I will pay more attention to ideological education."

"Good."

It seemed he didn't want to talk more, so I stood up and took my leave. Outside, the snow had stopped and the north wind turned colder. On my way back to my platoon, I felt bad, wondering how to handle the case. I was upset by Liu Fu. What a shame. I had always considered him as a candidate for an important job. His squad leader, Li Yaoping, was going to be demobilized the next year, and I had planned to have Liu Fu take over the squad. To be fair, Liu was in every way an excellent soldier. He surpassed all of my men in hand-grenade throwing. He could throw a grenade seventy-two meters. In our last practice with live ammunition, he scored eighty-four points with nine shots, which was higher than everybody except me. I got eighty-six. If we had a contest with the other three platoons, I would surely place him as our first man.

Needless to say, I liked him, not only for his ability and skills but also for his personality. He was a big fellow, over a hundred and eighty centimeters tall and a little heavily built but very nimble. His wide eyes reminded me of a small pony in my home village. In a way, his square mouth and bushy brows made him resemble those ancient generals in Spring Festival pictures. All the other soldiers liked him a lot too, and he had quite a few friends in our Ninth Company.

I can never forget how he became a figure of poetry. In the spring, when we sowed soybeans, I assigned the Third Squad to pull a plow, since we didn't have enough horses and oxen. On the first day the men were soaked with sweat and complained that it was animals' work. Though they sang some revolutionary songs and even pretended to be Japanese soldiers marching into a village, still there was no way of making the labor lighter. But the next day was different. Liu Fu and two other boys in the Third Squad appeared with bald heads. They said a bald head would make the sweating more endurable and the washing easier after the work. The atmosphere in the field came alive. The three shining round heads were wavering about like balloons at the front of the team. Everybody wanted to get some fun out of it. Because Liu Fu was taller and had a bigger head, he became the main target. In a few hours a poem was made in his honor, and the soldiers in the field chanted:

> When Big Liu takes off his hat,
> The county magistrate shakes his head:
> "Such a vast piece of alkaline land,
> How can the grain yield reach the Plan!"
>
> When Big Liu takes off his hat,
> The hardware store is so glad:

"With such a big shining bulb,
How many customers can we attract!"

When Big Liu takes off his hat,
The saleswoman is scared out of breath:
"Having sold condoms for so many years,
I've never seen such a length and breadth!"

In a few days the whole company learned the doggerel. Big
Liu was never offended by it. He even chanted it with others, but he would replace the name Big Liu with Small
Wang, Old Meng, and some others. As his popularity grew,
he was welcomed everywhere in the company. A boy like
him could be a very able leader of a squad or a platoon. This
was why I had planned to promote him to squad leader the
next year. But who could tell he was a "Flowery Fox."

Our Party secretary was right: There must have been a
pimp. Hutou was over fifty *li* away from Mati Mountain,
where we were garrisoned; at most Liu Fu had gone to the
county town seven or eight times on Sundays. He had seen
Little White Fairy six times? Almost every time he went
there? It was impossible, unless at the very beginning somebody took him directly to that woman. I remembered Li
Dong had gone with him for his first visit to the town, and
the second time Zhao Yiming had accompanied him. Both of
the older soldiers were reliable; it was unlikely that they
could be pimps. But to know a man's face is not to know his
heart. I had to question Liu Fu about this.

Our talk did not take long. He looked crestfallen and
ashamed, but he denied there had been somebody else involved and insisted to me that a good man must accept the
consequences of his own actions.

In a way, I appreciated his only blaming himself for the
whoring. If another man like him was found in my platoon,

I would have trouble clearing our name. People would chuckle and say the First Platoon had a whoring gang. That would give Liu Fu a hard time too, because he would surely be treated by the other men as a sort of traitor.

But I did take this case seriously, for I had to stop it. We stayed at the border to defend our country, and we must not lose our fighting spirit by chasing women. Unlike the Russians on the other side, we Chinese were revolutionary soldiers, and we could not rely on women to keep up our morale. Every Saturday night we saw from our watchtower the Russians having many college girls over in their barracks. They would sing and dance around bonfires, kiss and embrace in the open air, roll and fuck in the woods. They were barbarians and Revisionists, while we were Chinese and true Revolutionaries.

So I ordered Liu Fu to write out his self-criticism, examining the elements of bourgeois ideology in his brain and getting a clear understanding of the nature of his offense. He wept and begged me not to take disciplinary action against him. He was afraid his family would know it, and he would carry the stain for the rest of his life. I told him that a disciplinary action would have to be taken and that I was unable to help him with that. It was better to tell him the truth.

"So I'm done for?" His horsey eyes watched my mouth expectantly.

"Your case was sent down by the Regimental Political Department. You know our company cannot interfere with a decision from above. Usually, an offender like you *is* punished with a disciplinary action, but this doesn't mean you will have to carry it for the rest of your life. It depends on your own behavior. Say from now on you behave well in every way, you may have it taken out of your file when you are demobilized."

He opened his big mouth, but he didn't say anything, as if he swallowed down some words that had been stuck in his throat. The word *demobilized* must have struck him hard, because a soldier like him from the countryside would work diligently in order to be promoted to officer's rank. It would be a misfortune to return to his poor home village, where no job waited for him; if he had no job, no girl would marry him. But with such a stigma in his record, Liu Fu's future in the army was fixed: He would never be an officer.

Two days later he turned in his self-criticism. On eight white sheets were lines of big scrawled words and a few ink stains. A country boy like him of course couldn't say extraordinary things. His language was plain, and many sentences were broken. The gist of his self-criticism was that he had not worked hard enough to purge the bourgeois ideology from his head and that he had contracted the disease of liberalism. The Seventh Rule for the Army stated clearly: "Nobody is allowed to take liberties with women," but he had forgotten Chairman Mao's instruction and violated the rule. He also had forgotten his duty as a soldier staying on the Northern Frontier: When the enemies were sharpening their teeth and grinding their sabers at the border, he was indulging himself in sexual pleasure. He was unworthy of the nurture of the Party, unworthy of the Motherland's expectation, unworthy of his parents' efforts to raise him, unworthy of the gun that the people had entrusted to his hands, unworthy of his new green uniform.

I knew he was not a glib man, so I spared him the trouble of putting more self-scathing words in writing. His attitude was sincere; this alone counted.

He looked a little comforted when I told him that I would try to persuade Secretary Chang to ask the Regimental Political Department to administer less severe punishment to him. "This is not over yet," I warned him, "but you mustn't take it as a heavy burden. Try to turn over a new leaf and work hard to make up for it."

He said he was grateful and would never forget my help.

Two weeks passed. We had not heard anything from the Political Department about Liu Fu's case. Neither the Party secretary nor the company commander ever requested an action. It would be unwise to do that, because the longer we waited the more lenient the punishment would be. Time would take away the interest and the urgency of the case. In fact, none of the company leaders would welcome a severe action against Liu Fu. Liu was their man; no good leader would like to see his own man being punished.

A month passed, and still nothing happened. Liu Fu seemed very patient and was quieter than before. To prevent him from being involved with Little White Fairy again, we kept him at Mati Mountain on weekends. We were also strict about permitting other men, especially new soldiers, to visit Hutou Town.

One night it was my turn to make the rounds through all our sentry posts, checking the men on duty to make sure they didn't doze off. We had five posts, including the new one at the storehouse where we kept our food and a portion of our ammunition. I hated to do the supervision at midnight, when you had to jump out of bed and pretend to be as awake as a cat. If you didn't look spirited in front of them, the men on duty would follow your example and make no effort to stay awake.

I went to the parking yard first, where our trucks and mortars stood, and caught the sentry smoking in the dark. I ordered him to put out his cigarette. The boy complained it was too cold and he couldn't keep his eyelids apart if he had nothing to do. I told him that everybody had to stand his hours on cold nights. Nobody but the Lord of Heaven was to blame for the cold. As for his sleepiness, he'd better bear in mind that we were merely four *li* away from the Russians. If he didn't stay alert, he put his own neck at risk. The Russians often sent over their agents to find out our sentry positions and deployment. They would get rid of a sentry if they found it necessary and convenient. So for his own safety, he'd better keep his eyes open and not show them where he was.

Next I went to the gate post and our headquarters. Everything was fine at these two places. I chatted with each of the men for a few minutes and gave them some roasted sunflower seeds. Then I left for the storehouse.

The post was empty there, so I waited inside the house, believing the sentry must have been urinating or emptying his bowels somewhere outside.

After ten minutes nobody showed up. I began to worry and was afraid something unusual might have happened. I couldn't shout to summon the sentry over. That was the last thing you would do at night, because it would wake up the whole company and the Russians might hear it as well. But I had to find out where the soldier had hidden himself. He must have been dozing away somewhere. There were no disordered footprints in the snow; it was unlikely that he had been kidnapped or murdered. I picked up a line of footprints that looked new and followed it for a little distance. They were heading toward our stable. I raised my eyes and saw a dim light at the skylight on the stable's roof. Somebody must be there. What's he up to in the stable? Who is on duty? I looked at my luminous watch — 1:30 — and couldn't recall who the sentry was.

Getting close to the door, I heard some noise inside, so I hastened my steps. With my rifle I raised the cotton door curtain to take a look inside and make sure no one was hiding behind the door waiting to knock me down.

It was Liu Fu! He was standing beside our gray mule buckling his belt. His gun leaned against the long manger, and his fur hat hung on its muzzle. Beyond the mule stood a dozen horses, asleep with downcast heads. So he is the sentry. The rascal, he's using the stable as a latrine. How luxurious, keeping his butt warm in here.

No. I noticed something unusual. Behind the gray mule's hindquarters was a bench. On the bench there were some particles of snow and some wet smudges. The beast! He has been screwing the mule! Looking at him, I found his sweating face distorted with an awkward but clear expression, as if saying to me: *I can't help it, please, I can't help it!*

I sprang at him and grabbed him by the front of his jacket. Though he was much bigger and stronger than I was, I felt him go limp in my hand. Of course, a spent beast. I started slapping his face and cursing. "You — mule fucker! You never give your cock a break! I'll geld you today and throw your itchy balls to the dogs!"

He didn't resist and merely moaned, as if my cursing and slapping made him feel better. He looked so ashamed. Not encountering any resistance, I soon cooled down. You couldn't go on for long beating a man who didn't even raise his hands to defend himself. I let him go and ordered, "Back to the storehouse. We'll settle it tomorrow."

He picked up his gun, wiped away the tears on his cheeks with his hat, and went out quietly. In the stable all the animals were awake now, their eyes open and their ears raised. One horse snorted.

I couldn't wait for tomorrow and had Li Yaoping, Liu Fu's squad leader, awakened. We had to talk before I reported this to our Party secretary. I wanted to know more about Liu Fu.

It was understandable if you screwed a girl in the town, because there was no woman on the mountain. But to screw a dumb animal like that, who could imagine it! It nauseated me.

Li was not completely awake when he came into my room. I gave him a cigarette and struck a match for him. "Sit down. I want to talk with you."

He sat on a stool and began smoking. "What do you want to talk about on a dark — " He looked at his watch. "It's already half past two in the morning."

"I want to talk about Liu Fu. Just now I found him in the stable fooling around with the gray mule." I wouldn't say, "He screwed the mule," since I didn't see him do it. But I was sure of it, and Liu Fu himself had not denied it when I cursed and beat him. I was about to explain to Li what I meant.

"Oh no, you mean he did it again?" Li shook his freckled face.

"Yes. So you knew it already?"

"Ye-yes." He nodded.

"Why didn't you inform me of that before? Who gave you the right to hide it from me?" I was angry and would have yelled at him if some of my men had not been sleeping in the adjacent room.

"He promised me never to do it again." Li looked worried. "I thought I should give him a chance."

"A chance? Didn't we give him one when he was caught with Little White Fairy?" I felt outraged. Apparently this thing had been going on in my platoon for quite a while, but I had never got a whiff of it. "Tell me, when did you see him do it and how many times?"

"I saw him with the mule just once. It was last Saturday night. I saw him standing on a bench and hanging on the mule's hindquarters. I watched for a minute through the back window of the stable, then I coughed. He was scared and immediately fell off. When he saw me come in, he knelt down, begging me to forgive him and not to tell on him. He looked so piteous, a big fellow like that, so I told him I wouldn't tell. But I did criticize him."

"What did you say? How did you criticize him, my comrade squad leader?" I felt it strange that he took such pity on the man.

"I asked him why he had to screw the mule." Li looked rather cheerful.

"What a stupid question. How did he answer it?"

"He said, 'You know, Squad Leader, only — only mules don't foal. I promise, I'll never touch any — any of these mares.'" Li started tittering.

"What? It's absurd. You mean he thought he could get those mares with babies?"

"Yeah, yes!"

"What a silly fellow! So moral, he's afraid of being a father of horsey bastards." I couldn't help laughing, and Li's tittering turned into loud laughter too.

"Shhh." I reminded him of the sleepers.

"I told him even the mule must not be 'touched,' and he promised not to do it again." Li winked at me.

"Old Li, you're an old fox."

"Don't be so hard on me, my platoon leader. To be fair, he is a good boy in every way except that he can't control his lust. I don't know why. If you say he has too much bourgeois stuff in his head, that won't fit. He is from a pure poor peasant family, a healthy seedling on a red root —"

"I don't want you to work out a theory, Old Li. I want to know how we should handle him now. This morning, in a few hours, I will report this to our Company Headquarters. What should we say and how should we say it?"

"Well, do you want to get rid of him or keep him?"

This was indeed the crucial question, but I didn't have an answer. Liu Fu was my best man, and I would need him in the future. "What's your opinion then? At least we must not cover it up this time." I realized that Old Li hadn't told on Liu Fu because he wanted to keep him in his squad.

"Certainly, he had his chance already. How about —"

The door burst open and somebody rushed in. It was Ma Pingli, our youngest boy, who was to stand the three o'clock shift at the storehouse. "Platoon Leader, Liu Fu is not — not at the post." He took the fur cover off his nose, panting hard. "All the telephone wires are cut. We can't call anywhere."

"Did you go around and look for him?"

"Yes, everywhere."

"Where's his gun?"

"The gun is still there, in the post, but he's gone."

"Hurry up! Bring over the horses!" I ordered. "We'll go get him."

Ma ran away to the stable. I glanced at Old Li. The look on his face showed he understood what was happening. "Take this with you." I handed him a semiautomatic rifle, which he accepted absentmindedly, and I picked up another one for myself. In uneasy silence, we went out to wait for Ma.

The horses sweated all over, climbing toward the border. I calculated that we would have enough time to stop him before he could get across. He had to climb a long way from the southern side of the mountain to avoid being spotted by our watchtower. But when we reached the Wusuli River, a line of fresh footprints stretched before us, winding across the snow-covered surface of the river, extending itself to the other side, and gradually fading in the bluish whiteness of the vast Russian territory.

"The beast, stronger than a horse," I said. It was unimaginable that he could run so fast in the deep snow.

"He's there!" Ma Pingli pointed to a small slope partly covered by gray bushes.

Indeed, I saw a dark dot moving toward the edge of the thicket, which was about five hundred meters away from us. Impossible — surely he was too smart not to put on his camouflage cape. I raised my binoculars and saw him carrying a big stuffed gunnysack on his right shoulder and running desperately for the shelter of the bushes, the white cape secured around his neck flapping behind him like a huge butterfly. I gave the binoculars to Old Li.

Li watched. "He's taking a sack of *Forwards* with him!" he said with amazement.

"He stole it from the kitchen. I saw the kitchen door broken," Ma reported. We all knew our cooks stored *Forwards*, the newspaper of Shenyang Military Region, in gunnysacks as kindling. We had been told not to toss the paper about, because the Russians tried to get every issue of it in Hong Kong and would pay more than ten dollars for it.

"The Russians may not need those back issues at all," I said. "They've already got them. They only want recent ones. He's dumb."

Suddenly a yellow light pierced the sky over the slope. The Russians' lookout tower must have spotted him; their jeep was coming to pick him up.

Old Li and I looked at each other. We knew what we had to do. No time to waste. "We have no choice," I muttered, putting a sighting glass onto my rifle. "He has betrayed our country, and he is our enemy now."

I raised the rifle and aimed at him steadily. A burst of fire fixed him there. He collapsed in the distant snow, and the big sack fell off his shoulder and rolled down the slope.

"You got him!" Ma shouted.

"Yes, I got him. Let's go back."

We mounted the saddles; the horses immediately galloped down the mountain. They were eager to get out of the cold wind and return to their stable.

All the way back, none of us said another word.

Ocean of Words

Zhou Wen's last year in the People's Army was not easy. All his comrades pestered him, because in their eyes he was a bookworm, a scholar of sorts. Whenever they played poker, or chatted, or cracked jokes, he would sneak out to a place where he could read alone. This habit annoyed not only his fellow soldiers but also the chief of the Radio-telegram Station, Huang Peng, whose rank was equal to a platoon commander's. Chief Huang would say to his men, "This is not college. If you want to be a college student, you'd better go home first." Everybody knew he referred to Zhou.

The only thing they liked about Zhou was that he would work the shift they hated most, from 1:00 A.M. to 8:00 A.M. During the small hours Zhou read novels and middle school textbooks instead of the writings by Chairman Mao, Marx, Lenin, and Stalin. Often in the early morning he watched the eastern sky turn gray, pale, pink, and bright. The dawn was driving the night away from Longmen City bit by bit until, all of a sudden, a fresh daybreak descended, shining upon thousands of red roofs.

If not for the help of Director Liang Ming of the Divisional Logistics Department, Zhou's last year in the army would have been disastrous. Liang and his family lived in a grand church built by nineteenth-century Russian missionaries, which was at the southern corner of the Divisional Headquarters compound. A large red star stood atop the steeple. Within the church many walls had been knocked down to create a large auditorium, which served as the division's conference hall, movie house, and theater. All the fancy bourgeois pews had been pulled out and replaced by long proletarian benches, and Chairman Mao's majestic portrait had driven off the superstitious altarpiece.

The Liangs lived in the back of the church, as did the soldiers of the Radio-telegram Station. Because the antennas needed height, the radiomen occupied the attic, while the director's family had for themselves the three floors underneath. Whenever there was a movie on, the men at the station would steal into the auditorium through the rear door and sit against the wall, watching the screen from the back stage. They never bothered to get tickets. But except for those evenings when there were movies shown or plays performed, the back door would be locked. Very often Zhou dreamed of studying alone in the spacious front hall. Unable to enter it, he had to go outside to read in the open air.

One evening in October he was reading under a road lamp near the church. It was cloudy and a snow was gathering, just as the loudspeaker had announced that morning. Zhou was so engrossed he didn't notice somebody approaching until a deep voice startled him. "What are you doing here, little comrade?" Director Liang stood in front of Zhou, smiling kindly. His left sleeve, without an arm inside, hung listlessly from his shoulder, the cuff lodged in his pocket. His baggy eyes were fixed on Zhou's face.

"Reading," Zhou managed to say, closing the book and reluctantly showing him the title. He tried to smile but only twitched his lips, his eyes dim with fear.

"*The Three Kingdoms!*" Liang cried. He pointed at the other book under Zhou's arm. "How about this one?"

"*Ocean of Words*, a dictionary." Zhou regretted having taken the big book out with him.

"Can I have a look?"

Zhou handed it to the old man, who began flicking through the pages between the green covers. "It looks like a good book," Liang said and gave it back to Zhou. "Tell me, what's your name?"

"Zhou Wen."

"You're in the Radio Station upstairs, aren't you?"

"Yes."

"Do you often read old books?"

"Yes." Zhou was afraid the officer would confiscate the novel, which he had borrowed from a friend in the Telephone Company.

"Why don't you read inside?" Liang asked.

"It's noisy upstairs. They won't let me read in peace."

"Tickle their grandmothers!" Liang shook his gray head. "Follow me."

Unsure what was going on, Zhou didn't follow him. Instead he watched Liang's stout back moving away.

"I order you to come in," the director said loudly, opening the door to his home.

Zhou followed Liang to the second floor. The home was so spacious that the first floor alone had five or six rooms. Down the hall the red floor was shiny under the chandelier; the brown windowsill at the stairway was large enough to be a bed. Liang opened a door and said, "You use this room. Whenever you want to study, come here and study inside."

"This, this —"

"I order you to use it. We have lots of rooms. From now on, if I see you reading outside again, I will kick all of you out of this building."

189

"No, no, they may want me at any time. What should I say if they can't find me?"

"Tell them I want you. I want you to study and work for me here." Liang closed the door, and his leather boots thumped away downstairs.

Outside, snowflakes suddenly began fluttering to the ground. Through the window Zhou saw the backyard of the small grocery that was run by some officers' wives. A few naked branches were tossing, almost touching the panes. Inside, green curtains covered the corners of the large window. Though bright and clean, the room seemed to be used as a repository for old furniture. On the floor was a large desk, a stool, a chair, a wooden bed standing on its head against the wall, and a rickety sofa. But for Zhou this was heaven. Full of joy, he read three chapters that evening.

Soon the downstairs room became Zhou's haven. In the Radio Company he could hardly get along with anybody; there was a lot of ill feeling between him and his leaders and comrades. He tried forgetting all the unhappy things by making himself study hard downstairs, but that didn't always help. His biggest headache was his imminent discharge from the army: not the demobilization itself so much as his non-Party status. It was obvious that without Communist Party membership he wouldn't be assigned a good job once he returned home. Thinking him bookish, the Party members in the Radio Company were reluctant to consider his application seriously. Chief Huang would never help him; neither would Party Secretary Si Ma Lin. Zhou had once been on good terms with the secretary; he had from time to time helped Si Ma write articles on current political topics and chalked up slogans and short poems on the large blackboard in front of the Company Headquarters. That broad piece of wood was the company's face, because it was the first thing a visitor would see and what was on it displayed the men's sincere political attitudes and lofty aspirations. The secretary had praised Zhou three times for the poems and calligraphy on the blackboard, but things had gone bad between Zhou and Si Ma because of *Ocean of Words*.

The dictionary was a rare book, which Zhou's father had bought in the early 1950s. It was compiled in 1929, was seven by thirteen inches in size and over three thousand pages thick, and had Chinese, Latin, and English indexes. Its original price was eighty silver dollars, but Zhou's father had paid a mere one *yuan* for it at a salvage station, where all things were sold by weight. The book weighed almost three *jin*. Having grown up with the small *New China Dictionary*, which had only a few thousand entries, Secretary Si Ma had never imagined there was such a big book in the world. When he saw it for the first time, he browsed through the pages for two hours, pacing up and down in his office with the book in his arms as if cradling a baby. He told Zhou, "I love this book. What a treasure. It's a gold mine, an armory!"

One day at the Company Headquarters the secretary asked Zhou, "Can I have that great book, Young Zhou?"

"It's my family's heirloom. I can't give it to anybody." Zhou regretted having shown him the dictionary and having even told him that his father had spent only one *yuan* for it.

"I won't take it for free. Give me a price. I'll pay you a good sum."

"Secretary Si Ma, I can't sell it. It's my father's book."

"How about fifty *yuan*?"

"If it were mine I would give it to you free."

"A hundred?"

"No, I won't sell."

"Two hundred?"

"No."

"You are a stubborn, Young Zhou, you know." The secretary looked at Zhou with a meaningful smile.

From that moment on, Zhou knew that as long as Si Ma was the Party secretary in the company, there would be no hope of his joining the Party. Sometimes he did think of giving him the dictionary, but he could not bear to part with it. After he had refused Si Ma's request for the second time, his mind could no longer remain at ease; he was afraid somebody would steal the book the moment he didn't have it with him. There was no safe place to hide it at the station; his comrades might make off with it if they knew the secretary would pay a quarter of his yearly salary for it. Fortunately, Zhou had his own room now, so he kept the dictionary downstairs in a drawer of the desk.

One evening as Zhou was reading in the room, Director Liang came in, followed by his wife carrying two cups. "Have some tea, Little Zhou?" Liang said. He took a cup and sat down on the sofa, which began squeaking under him.

Zhou stood up, receiving the cup with both hands from Mrs. Liang. "Please don't do this for me."

"Have some tea, Little Zhou," she said with a smile. She looked very kind, her face covered with wrinkles. "We are neighbors, aren't we?"

"Yes, we are."

"Sit down, and you two talk. I have things to do downstairs." She turned and walked away.

"Don't be so polite. If you want tea, just take it," Liang said, blowing away the tea leaves in his cup. Zhou took a sip.

"Little Zhou," Liang said again, "you know I like young people who study hard."

"Yes, I know."

"Tell me, why do you want to study?"

"I don't know for sure. My grandfather was a scholar, but my father didn't finish middle school. He joined the Communist Army to fight the Japanese. He always wants me to study hard and says we are a family of scholars and must carry on the tradition. Besides, I like reading and writing."

"Your father is a good father," Liang announced, as if they were at a meeting. "I'm from a poor peasant's family. If a carrying pole stood up on the ground, my father couldn't tell it means 'one.' But I always say the same thing to my kids like your father says. You see, nowadays schools are closed. Young people don't study but make revolution outside school. They don't know a fart about the revolution. For the revolutionary cause I lost my arm and these fingers." He raised his only hand, whose little and ring fingers were missing. The stumps quivered in the fluorescent light.

Zhou nerved himself for the question. "Can I ask how you lost your arm?"

"All right, I'm going to tell you the story, so that you will study harder." Liang lifted the cup and took a gulp. The tea gargled in his mouth for a few seconds and then went down. "In the fall of 1938, I was a commander of a machine-gun company in the Red Army, and we fought against Chiang Kai-shek's troops in a mountain area in Gansu. My company's task was to hold a hilltop. From there you could control two roads with machine guns. We took the hill and held it to protect our retreating army. The first day we fought a battle with two enemy battalions that attempted to take the hill from us. They left about three hundred bodies on the slopes, but our Party secretary and sixteen other men were killed. Another twenty were badly wounded. Night came, and we had no idea if all of our army had passed and how long we had to stay on the hill. At about ten o'clock, an orderly came from the Regimental Staff and delivered a message. It had only two words penciled on a scrap of paper. I could tell it was Regimental Commander Hsiao Hsiong's bold handwriting.

"I turned the paper up and down, left and right, but couldn't figure out the meaning. I shouted to the whole company, 'Who can read?' Nobody answered. In fact, only the Party secretary could read, but we had lost him. You can imagine how outraged I was. We were all blind with good eyes! I beat my head with my fists and couldn't stop cursing. Grabbing the messenger's throat, I yelled, 'If you don't tell me what the message is, I'll shoot you in the eye!'

"The platoon leaders saved the boy's life. They told me it wasn't his fault; he couldn't read either. And a messenger never knew the contents of a message, because if he was caught by the enemy they could make him tell them what he knew. Usually, he was ordered to swallow the message before it fell into the enemy's hands.

"What should we do now? We had no idea where our army was, although we had been told that if we retreated we should go to Maliang Village. That was twenty *li* away in the north. Racking our brains together, we figured there could be only two meanings in the message; one was to stay and the other to retreat, but we couldn't decide which was the one. If the message said to stay but we retreated, then the next day, when our troops passed the mountain without covering fire, there would be heavy casualties and I would be shot by the higher-ups. If the message said to retreat but we stayed, we merely took a risk. That meant to fight more battles or perhaps lose contact with our army for some time afterwards. After weighing the advantages and disadvantages, I decided to stay and told my men to sleep so we could fight the next day. Tired out, we all slept like dead pigs."

Zhou almost laughed, but he restrained himself. Liang went on, "At about five in the morning, the enemy began shelling us. We hadn't expected they would use heavy artillery. The day before they had only launched some mortar shells. Within a minute, rocks, machine guns, arms and legs, branches and trunks of trees were flying everywhere. I heard bugles buzzing on all sides below. I knew the enemy had surrounded us and was charging. At least two thirds of my men were already wiped out by the artillery — there was no way to fight such a battle. I shouted, 'Run for your lives, brothers!' and led my orderly and a dozen men running away from the hilltop. The enemy was climbing all around. Machine guns were cracking. We had only a few pistols with us — no way to fight back. We were just scrambling for our lives. A shell exploded at our rear and killed seven of the men following me. My left arm was smashed. These two fingers were cut off by a piece of shrapnel from that shell." Liang raised his crippled hand to the level of his collarbone. "Our regiment was at Maliang Village when we arrived. Regimental Commander Hsiao came and slapped my face while the medical staff were preparing to saw my arm off. I didn't feel anything; I almost blacked out. Later I was told that the words in the message were 'Retreat immediately.' If I hadn't lost this arm, Commander Hsiao would've finished me off on the spot. The whole company and twenty-two heavy machine guns, half the machine guns our regiment had, were all gone. Commander Hsiao punished me by making me a groom for the Regimental Staff. I took care of horses for six years. You see, Little Zhou, just two small words, each of them cost sixty lives. Sixty lives! It's a bloody lesson, a bloody lesson!" Liang shook his gray head and drank up the tea.

"Director Liang, I will always remember this lesson." Zhou was moved. "I understand now why you want us to study hard."

"Yes, you're a good young man, and you know the value of

books and knowledge. To carry out the revolution we must have literacy and knowledge first."

"Yes, we must."

"All right, it's getting late. I must go. Stay as long as you want. Remember, come and study every day. Never give up. A young man must have a high aspiration and then pursue it."

From then on, Zhou spent more time studying in the room. In the morning, when he was supposed to sleep, he would doze for only an hour and then read for three hours downstairs. His comrades wondered why his bed was empty every morning. When they asked where he had been, he said that Director Liang had work for him to do and that if they needed him, just give the Liangs a ring. Of course, none of them dared go down to check or call the director's home.

Now the "study" was clean and more furnished. The floor was mopped every day. On the desk sat a cup and a thermos bottle always filled with boiled water. Liang's orderly took care of that. Occasionally, the director would come and join Zhou in the evenings. He wanted Zhou to tell him the stories in *The Three Kingdoms*, which in fact Liang knew quite well, for he had heard them time and again for decades. Among the five generals in the classic, he adored Guan Yu, because Guan had both bravery and strategy. After *The Three Kingdoms*, they talked of *All Men Are Brothers*. Liang had Zhou tell him the stories of those outlaw heroes, which Liang actually knew by heart; he was just fond of listening to them. Whenever a battle took a sudden turn, he would give a hearty laugh. Somehow Zhou felt the old man looked younger during these evenings — pink patches would appear on his sallow cheeks after they had sat together for an hour.

Naturally Zhou became an enigma to his comrades, who

were eager to figure out what he did downstairs. One afternoon Chief Huang had a talk with Zhou. He asked, "Why do you go to Director Liang's home so often, Young Zhou?"

"I work for him." Zhou would never reveal that he studied downstairs, because the chief could easily find a way to keep him busy at the station.

"What work exactly?"

"Sometimes little chores, and sometimes he wants me to read out Chairman Mao's works and newspaper to him."

"Really? He studies every day?"

"Yes, he studies hard."

"How can you make me believe you?"

"Chief Huang, if you don't believe me, go ask him yourself." Zhou knew the chief dared not make a peep before the director. Huang had better keep himself away from Liang, or the old man would curse his ancestors of eight generations.

"No, it's unnecessary. Zhou Wen, you know I'm not interested in what you do downstairs. It's Secretary Si Ma Lin who asked me about what's going on. I have no idea how he came to know you often stay in Director Liang's home."

"Thanks for telling me that, Chief Huang. Please tell Secretary Si Ma that Director Liang wants me to work for him."

After that, the chief never bothered Zhou again, but Zhou's fellow comrades didn't stop showing their curiosity. They even searched through his suitcase and turned up his mattress to see what he had hidden from them. Zhou realized how lucky it was that he had put his *Ocean of Words* downstairs beforehand. They kept asking him questions. One would ask, "How did you get so close to Director Liang?" Another, "Does he pay you as his secretary?" Another would sigh and say, "What a pity Old Liang doesn't have a daughter!"

It was true Director Liang had only three sons. The eldest son was an officer in Nanjing Military Region; the second worked as an engineer at an ordnance factory in Harbin; his youngest son, Liang Bin, was a middle school student at home. The boy, tall and burly, was a wonderful soccer player. One afternoon during their break from the telegraphic training, Zhou Wen, Zhang Jun, and Gu Wan were playing soccer in the yard behind the church when Liang Bin came by. Bin put down his satchel, hooked up the ball with his instep, and began juggling it on his feet, then on his head, on his shoulders, on his knees — every part of his body seemed to have a spring. He went on doing this for a good three minutes without letting the ball touch the ground. The soldiers were all impressed and asked the boy why he didn't play for the Provincial Juvenile Team.

"They've asked me many times," Bin said, "but I never dare play for them."

"Why?" Gu asked.

"If I did, my dad would break my legs. He wants me to study." He picked up his satchel and hurried home.

Both Zhang and Gu said Director Liang was a fool and shouldn't ruin his son's future that way. Zhou understood why, but he didn't tell them, uncertain if Director Liang would like other soldiers to know his story, which was profound indeed but not very glorious.

Every day the boy had to return home immediately after school, to study. One evening Zhou overheard Director Liang criticizing his son. "Zhou Wen read *The Three Kingdoms* under the road lamp. You have everything here, your own lamp, your own books, your own desk, and your own room. What you lack is your own strong will. Your mother has spoiled you. Come on, work on the geometry problems. I'll give you a big gift at the Spring Festival if you study hard."

"Will you allow me to join the soccer team?"

"No, you study."

A few days later, Director Liang asked Zhou to teach his son, saying that Zhou was the most knowledgeable man he had ever met and that he trusted him as a young scholar. Zhou agreed to try his best. Then Liang pulled a dog-eared book out of his pocket. "Teach him this," he said. It was a copy of *The Three-Character Scripture.*

Zhou was surprised, not having expected the officer wanted him to teach his son classical Chinese, which Zhou had merely taught himself a little. Where did Liang get this small book? Zhou had heard of the scripture but never seen a copy. Why did a revolutionary officer like Liang want his son to study such a feudal book? Zhou dared not ask and kept the question to himself. Neither did he ever mention the scripture to his comrades. Instead he told them that Director Liang ordered him to teach his son Chairman Mao's *On Practice,* a booklet Zhou knew well enough to talk about in their political studies. Since none of his comrades understood the Chairman's theory, they believed what Zhou told them, and they were impressed by his comments when they studied together.

As his demobilization drew near, Zhou worried desperately and kept asking himself, What will you do now? Without the Party membership you won't get a good job at home, but how can you join the Party before leaving the army? There are only five weeks left. If you can't make it by the New Year, you'll never be able to in the future. Even if you give the dictionary to Secretary Si Ma now, it's already too late. Too late to do anything. But you can't simply sit back waiting for the end; you must do something. There must be a way to bring him around. How?

After thinking of the matter for three days, he decided to talk to Director Liang. One evening, as soon as Zhou sat down in the room, the old man rushed in with snowflakes on his felt hat. "Little Zhou," he said in a thick voice, "I came to you for help."

"How can I help?" Zhou stood up.

"Here, here is Marx's book." Liang put his fur mitten on the desk and pulled a copy of *Manifesto of the Communist Party* out of it. "This winter we divisional leaders are studying this little book. Vice Commissar Hou gave the first lecture this afternoon. I don't understand what he said at all. It wasn't a good lecture. Maybe he doesn't understand Marx either."

"I hope I can help."

"For example," Liang said, putting the book on the desk and turning a few pages, "here, listen: 'An apparition — an apparition of Communism — has wandered throughout Europe.' Old Hou said an apparition is a 'spook.' Europe was full of spooks. I wonder if it's true. What's an 'apparition,' do you know?"

"Let's see what it means exactly." Zhou took his *Ocean of Words* out of the drawer and began to turn the pages.

"This must be a treasure book, having all the rare characters in it," Liang said, standing closer to watch Zhou searching for the word.

"Here it is." Zhou lifted the dictionary and read out the definition: "'Apparition — specter, ghost, spiritual appearance.'"

"See, no 'spook' at all."

"'Spook' may not be completely wrong for 'apparition,' but it's too low a word."

"You're right. Good. Tomorrow I'll tell Old Hou to drop his 'spook.' By the way, I still don't understand why Marx calls Communism 'an operation.' Isn't Communism a good ideal?"

Zhou almost laughed out loud at Liang's mispronunciation, but controlled himself and said, "Marx must be ironic here, because the bourgeoisie takes the Communists as poisonous snakes and wild beasts — something like an apparition."

"That's right." Liang slapped his paunch, smiling and shaking his head. "You see, Little Zhou, my mind always goes straight and never makes turns. You're a smart young man. I regret I didn't meet you earlier."

Here came Zhou's chance. He said, "But we can't be together for long, because I'll leave for home soon. I'm sure I will miss you and this room."

"What? You mean you'll be discharged?"

"Yes."

"Why do they want a good soldier like you to go?"

Zhou told the truth. "I want to leave the army myself, because my old father is in poor health."

"Oh, I'm sorry you can't stay longer."

"I will always be grateful to you."

"Anything I can do for you before you leave?"

"One thing, though I don't know if it's right to mention."

"Just say it. I hate men who mince words. Speak up. Let's see if this old man can be helpful." Liang sat down on the sofa.

Zhou pulled over the chair and sat on it. "I'm not a Party member yet. It's shameful."

"Why? Do you know why they haven't taken you into the Party?"

"Yes, because my comrades think I have read too much and I am different from them."

"What?" The thick eyebrows stood up on Liang's forehead. "Does Secretary Si Ma Lin have the same opinion?"

"Yes, he said I had some stinking airs of a petty intellectual. You know I didn't even finish middle school."

"The bastard, I'll talk to him right now. Come with me." Liang went out to the corridor, where a telephone hung on the wall. Zhou was scared but had to follow him. He regretted having blurted out what the secretary had said and was afraid Director Liang would ask Si Ma what he meant by "stinking airs of a petty intellectual."

"Give me Radio Company," Liang grunted into the phone.

"Hello, who's this? . . . I want to speak to Si Ma Lin." Liang turned to Zhou. "I must teach this ass a lesson."

"Hello," he said into the phone again. "Is that you, Little Si Ma? . . . Sure, you can tell my voice. Listen, I have a serious matter to discuss with you. . . . It's about Zhou Wen's Party membership. He is a young friend of mine. I have known him for a while and he is a good soldier, a brilliant young man. For what reason haven't you accepted him as a Party member? Isn't he going to leave soon?"

He listened to the receiver. Then he said out loud, "What? The devil take you! That's exactly why he can be a good Party member. What time are we in now? — the seventies of the twentieth century — and you are still so hostile to a knowledgeable man. You still have a peasant's mind. Why does he have to stand the test longer than others? Only because he's learned more? You have a problem in your brain, you know. Tell me, how did we Communists defeat Chiang Kai-shek? With guns? Didn't he have American airplanes and tanks? How come our army, with only rifles plus millet, beat his eight million troops equipped with modern weapons?"

The smart secretary was babbling his answer at the other end. Zhou felt a little relieved, because the director hadn't mentioned what he had told him.

"That's rubbish!" Liang said. "We defeated him by having the Pen. Old Chiang only had the Gun, but we had both the Gun and the Pen. As Chairman Mao has taught us: The Gun and the Pen, we depend on both of them to make revolution and cannot afford to lose either. Are you not a Party secretary? Can't you understand this simple truth? You have a problem here, don't you?"

The clever secretary seemed to be admitting his fault, because the old man sounded less scathing now. "Listen, I don't mean to give you a hard time. I'm an older soldier, and my Party membership is longer than your age, so I know what kind of people our Party really needs. We can recruit men who carry guns by the millions, easily. What we want badly is those who carry pens. My friend Zhou Wen is one of them, don't you think? . . . Comrade Si Ma Lin, don't limit your field of vision to your own yard. Our revolutionary cause is a matter of the entire world. Zhou Wen may not be good in your eyes, but to our revolutionary cause, he is good and needed. Therefore, I suggest you consider his application seriously. . . . Good, I'm pleased you understood it so quickly. . . . Good-bye now." Liang hung up and said to Zhou, "The ass, he's so dense." Zhou was sweating, his heart thumping.

Director Liang's call cleared away all obstacles. Within two weeks Zhou joined the Party. Neither Secretary Si Ma nor Chief Huang said a word alluding to the call. It seemed the secretary had not divulged to anybody the lesson he had received on the telephone. Certainly Zhou's comrades were amazed by the sudden breakthrough, and he became more mysterious in their eyes. It was rumored that Zhou wouldn't be discharged and instead would be promoted to officer's rank and do propaganda work in the Divisional Political Department. But that never materialized.

The day before he left the army, Zhou went downstairs to fetch his things and say good-bye to Director Liang. No sooner had he entered the room than the old man came in holding something in his hand. It was a small rectangular box covered with purple satin. Liang placed it on the desk and said, "Take this as a keepsake."

Zhou picked it up and opened the lid — a brown Hero pen perched in the white cotton groove. On its chunky body was a vigorous inscription carved in golden color: "For Comrade Zhou Wen — May You Forever Hold Tight the Revolutionary Pen, Liang Ming Present."

"I appreciate your helping my son," the old man said.

Too touched to say a word, Zhou put the pen into his pocket. Though he had taught the boy *The Three-Character Scripture,* Liang had helped him join the Party, which was an important event in anyone's life, like marriage or rebirth. Even without this gift, Zhou was the one who was indebted, so now he had to give something in return. But he didn't have any valuables with him. At this moment it dawned on him that his *Ocean of Words* was in the drawer. He took it out and presented it to Liang with both hands. "You may find this useful, Director Liang."

"Oh, I don't want to rob you of your inheritance. You told me it's your father's book." Liang was rubbing his hand on his leg.

"Please keep it. My father will be glad if he knows it's in your hands."

"All right, it's a priceless treasure." Liang's three fingers were caressing the solid spine of the tome. "I'll cherish it and make my son read ten pages of this good book every day."

Zhou was ready to leave. Liang held out his hand; for the first time Zhou shook that crippled hand, which was ice cold.

"Good-bye," Liang said, looking him in the eye. "May you have a bright future, Little Zhou. Study hard and never give up. You will be a great man, a tremendous scholar. I just know that in my heart."

"I will study hard. Take good care of yourself, Director Liang. I'll write to you. Good-bye."

The old man heaved a feeble sigh and waved his hand. Zhou walked out, overwhelmed by the confidence and resolution surging up in his chest. Outside, the air seemed to be gleaming, and the sky was blue and high. Up there, in the distance, two Chinese jet fighters were soaring noiselessly, ready to knock down any intruder. It was at this moment that Zhou made up his mind to become a socialist man of letters, fighting with the Revolutionary Pen for the rest of his life.